# ENTICED BY A HOODLUM

### SWEET TEE

Enticed by a Hoodlum
Copyright 2019 by Sweet Tee

Published by Mz. Lady P Presents

All rights reserved

# ACKNOWLEDGMENTS

I am grateful for all of the opportunities that have come my way. I continue to pray for many blessings to fall in my lap. Thank you, supporters, and readers. Thank you for reading my work, sharing a link, or suggesting my book to someone. Special thanks to my mentors who I will not name for the continuous support and encouragement.

Thank you, Boss Lady, aka, Patrice Williams, better known as National Best Selling Author, Mz. Lady P. You have guided, encouraged, and never given up on me, and I appreciate it. For two years, I have learned so much as an author from you on how to promote and brand myself. Your hard work and dedication do not go unnoticed, nor do I take you for granted. I look forward to growing and becoming the dopiest author I can be under your company. You are stuck with me FOREVER! LOL. You are a beast in this industry so to be a part of your team is a wonderful feeling. Thank you for seeing the potential in me during a difficult time in my life.

Shout out to my dope pen sisters. Our family is growing and glowing with talent across the board. I'm proud of you all. Thank you for always keeping it real and for providing advice and motivation. This is book # 7 y'all! It's an amazing feeling to add to my book collection. I want to thank my mother as she watches from heaven and continues to give me inspiration. There is not one day that goes by that I do not think about you. You inspire some of my crazy characters from the stories that you used to share about back in the day. Continue to watch over your son and me.

To those who have a dream, follow it and never give up! Push through, and if you want it bad enough, your hard work will pay off. The stories I write always have some type of message to it, and it is my sincere hope that it inspires the readers. Living the life we were dealt is easier said than done for some folks. Therefore, it is nice to get lost in others' drama via a good book. Each character created is based on friends, old associates, and from people watching.

Lastly, I would like to acknowledge myself for fighting against depression. Each day is a challenge, especially during November and December. The loss of a mother is a hard pill to swallow. Depression can consume and turn you into a different person unless you fight it! I write to cope, I write to inspire, and I write to promote my story.

Love yours truly,
~Sweet Tee

# KEEP UP WITH SWEET TEE

FACEBOOK: AUTHORESS SWEET TEE

**Readers Group: Sweet Tee's Reading Corner**
**Instagram: sweettee3215**
**Twitter: AuthoressSweetT**
**Website: http://jonestt25.wixsite.com/sweettee**

# SYNOPSIS

Lani Kingston is the niece of a well-known drug supplier and has all of the material things a girl could ever want. Her uncle and five male cousins spoiled her rotten but didn't entertain the notion of dating. As a twenty-three-year-old woman, she did as she pleases testing her family at times. Her rebellion acts only served as a cry for help. One only a woman could understand.

Lenox Scott tried to leave the streets a thing of his past, able to walk away alive and without any jail time. Older and mature, he changed his lifestyle for the better. However, a situation involving his father brought him back to the city that he used to call home. A temporary stay lasted longer than expected, and he eventually learns the reasons why.

One day Lani and Lenox met at a food spot going as far as exchanging digits. Neither believed in love at first sight, but they definitely felt sparks fly. Over time, the pair established a friendship that turned intimate. Enticed in a way neither expected by one another, their actions brought about consequences, which further complicates things for both families. Once the Pandora box is opened, will Lani and Lenox remain lovers or turn into enemies?

# ONE

# LANI KINGSTON

Imagine having the best day ever at Chuck E. Cheese eating pizza, cake, and ice cream, just living your best life with no cares in the world, just pure innocent fun where children could be children. Life was simple because I had loving parents who got me everything I wanted and needed. However, within a matter of hours, life as I knew it changed forever, and I became an orphan. My Uncle Kingston took me into his home despite my unwillingness to be there. When I was no more than six-years-old, my parents were killed in an ambush on the orders of a rival drug lord. He went by the name Black on the streets and was well known for shooting somebody if they blinked at him wrong. I can remember it like it was yesterday, a thought that had been forever engraved in my brain. At first, I blamed my uncle for involving my parents in his lifestyle. However, it wasn't until I grew older that I learned the truth.

My name is Lani Kingston, the niece of a well-known drug supplier Kingston Sr. It was a big adjustment for us all when I moved in with my uncle and his five sons. Not used to so many people under one roof, I learned how to function living with all men. We moved into a mansion located in the Water Tower district on the east side of

Milwaukee. Uncle Kingston made sure that I had my own wing equipped with access to the indoor pool. Of course, he spoiled me rotten, but it didn't come without a price.

By age eleven, I had grown into a tomboy climbing fences as practice to run from police. I also played basketball in the Klotsche Center at UW-Milwaukee with my cousins, but they made me quit once the boys started noticing me. Most importantly, each of them trained me daily on how to protect myself and how to read the men that I encountered.

Kingsley taught me how to think strategically and made sure I knew the basic rules of law. He was the oldest, also our family attorney. Keenan, the second oldest, taught me how to read nonverbal behavior in detail. He owned a barbershop in Chicago and helped clean family money. Kaden got me hooked on shopping and fashion. Kaine and Kofi Jr. roughed me up and trained me how to take a punch and give one. It felt like a boot camp school for surviving the streets.

I remember my first challenge at age fifteen during one of Uncle Kingston's sit-downs at his warehouse. That was the first time I'd ever been in a room with so many well-dressed black men who held power. My task was to engage with each leader, size them up, and find out who the thief and rat were in the room.

I pushed a little cooler filled with bottles of Fiji water around the table and placed a bottle in from of them. Then I leaned over and whispered, "Did you hear what my uncle did to Stacey for stealing? I sure hope none of y'all were involved."

Their reactions to my words gave me the vibe and gut feeling on who the two untrustworthy niggas were who sat amongst the real riders. My gut-o-meter went haywire by the time I reached a bald dude who resembled Suge Knight. That shit turned me off instantly, not to mention the vibe. I didn't even need to say much to him as I continued to maneuver around to the last three. Afterwards, I sat and observed the men from afar one last time before sending my uncle a message with the men he needed to handle.

Uncle Kingston stood at the head of the rectangle glass table with his head down. I assumed he had been reading my message because he turned his head in my direction. A quick head nod was a sign of my certainty, but my young eyes weren't ready for what happened next. On that day, I truly understood why niggas feared my family as I watched the Suge Knight look-a-like get pistol-whipped, have his fingers cut off with a small hatchet, and then a hollow point went through his head. Unable to witness anymore, I vanished only to have my ride or die follow me.

Out of all my cousins, Kofi Jr. and I were thick as thieves, and he helped me adjust to the crime and murder that revolved around my life. My favorite cousin even had his girlfriend have the female talk when I got my period. It was because of my family that I had no choice but to boss up, gain thick skin, and have a strong stomach. The shit they did wasn't for the weak, and I loved my family for everything they did for me daily.

Still wet behind the ear, I had a lot of shit to learn about the streets, more specifically the men who ran in them. Uncle Kingston felt that I was ready to play a more constant role in the family business. My skills in reading people served helpful during important deals and meetings. In order to perfect my craft, he paid my tuition at UW-Milwaukee for psychology classes. My interest in people and their actions drove me to inquire more knowledge, and in return used my practical lessons to help my uncle weed out the bad apples in the barrow. My lovely boyfriend Justin served as a Guinea pig because I could read his every facial expression or movement.

After the first year, the coursework grew challenging yet exciting at the same time. Although I enjoyed the benefits of having a rich uncle who cared about my education, I sometimes hated the results that led to someone losing their life. As a female who lived with six men, I learned how to get what I wanted most of the time. The lie detector family gig wore on my conscious, so I found a clinical job at St. Joseph's Hospital. In doing so, my uncle allowed me to leave the mansion four days per week. It was refreshing to have a job and a boyfriend. Life had finally worked out for the best. Living without parents proved to be tougher than expected. However, no one could prepare me for the events that followed.

It wasn't easy living in a predominantly male family known as the Kingston Crew. They controlled eighty percent of the cocaine that moved through Milwaukee and Chicago. Life was far from normal for me because of their operation. However, I always kept money on me, owned a 2016 Mercedes Benz SUV, and wore any designer I dreamed. What else could a woman ask for, right?

The more I matured, the more I favored my mother, which made me shed tears often. Growing up without a mom or dad was a void that could never be replaced, but Uncle Kofi did his best to make sure I never wanted for anything. I had a five-thousand-dollar stipend per month. Like a princess of the clan, my bedroom was in my own wing of the mansion for privacy. However, it was really to keep me from knowing too much about the business.

By senior year high school, I switched from the tomboy phase to a more girly look, dresses, and a little makeup. When guys started to pay attention to me, my cousins always shut them down. They were super protective like brothers typically were. That is when the bond with each cousin got stronger, and my curiousness about my parents resurfaced. Kofi Jr., who was only five years older than I was, used to tell me shit that answered some of the questions I had. He explained how both my mom and dad were willing participants, got greedy, and was killed over it. Not old enough to understand at the time, most of my memories were of happy times and gifts. Rarely did I witness them argue, see drugs, or witness strangers entering our home.

My cousins were in the drug business, but each one earned a high school and college degree or higher. It was never a dull moment with them around because somebody was always getting shot at, beat up, or killed. No matter the case, they guarded my life, and I loved them for it. They got on my last nerve but that's what family did, and they were all I had.

I recall one time where Kofi Jr., Kaine, and I went to Checkers for some burgers and shakes, and this one chick tried to talk to Kofi Jr. The trick got mad because he turned her hood rat ass down and tried to call her brothers who were at a store nearby. We Kingston's didn't believe in running or stepping down from a fight. Three slinky ass dudes came running up only to catch a bullet to the chest; their bodies hit the pavement instantly. Instead of leaving, we waited for our food then proceeded to leave the establishment, and not one person said a word to us either. Welcome to the world of the Kingston crew.

# TWO

# LANI KINGSTON

Pissed that I had to work first and second shift at St. Joseph's, all my Valentine's Day plans went down the drain. My hair was fucked, nails were bogus, and all I wanted to do was smoke a fat blunt and go to sleep. By the time I clocked out, put on my coat, and exited out the door, there stood Justin. We had been an item since we were fourteen years old. Many said we were too young to be in love, but we ignored all the negative stuff people spoke. I loved Justin with all my heart, so much that we moved in together and planned our future.

Whenever I had to work late, he made sure to meet me outside of my job. He never liked me out alone when it got dark outside. I always told him it's a hospital. We save lives, so I'll be good. On that night, he stood before me dressed in a midnight blue suit, which made me feel even more like a bum.

"Hey baby," he greeted followed by a kiss on the forehead.

"Damn bae, you're dressed to kill tonight. I'm sorry about work, but a co-worker decided not to show up during shift change. I feel bad our night got ruined. How can I make it up to you?" Still, in front of the entrance, he reached inside his pocket and pulled out a small black velvet box he held cuffed in his left hand. Then he cleared his throat before kneeling on one knee.

"Oh my fucking goodness, Justin! You are not about to ask me…" I went speechless as I watched Justin open the box. Never had I seen a light displayed in a box that shined down on the three-carat diamond ring.

"Lani Monet Kingston, I knew from the first time we met that we'd end up together. You make me smile inside and out. I love everything about you, even on the days that you cuss my ass out. You can never do wrong in my eyes, I'm aware we still gotta face your family, but I'm asking you first. Will you marry me?"

Regardless of looking a hot mess and crying tears of joy, I knew Justin truly loved me. To some nineteen was a little young to get married, but if it's true love, the act should be acceptable. My family didn't approve of my dating but raised up for Justin who they deemed suitable for me to date. Marriage was an entirely different subject that I didn't look forward to discussing.

"YES!" I exclaimed with excitement as he slid the ring on my finger. The second he stood to his feet, we shared a passionate kiss and made our way to the parking lot. Not even ten steps away from our vehicles, the silhouette of two men dressed in all black appeared. They moved in quickly on Justin, and before we could get the car doors opened, the loud sounds erupted.

*POP! POP!*

"NOOO!" I screamed as the gunshots left me paralyzed, frozen in my stance. I watched the two bastards run off not able to rob us if that was their motive. Justin's body dropped and laid on the jet-black tar parking lot. I dropped down to my knees in search for a pulse, trying to locate the gunshot wounds.

Suddenly, a group of people surrounded the scene trying to figure out what happened. Someone had run inside to seek medical assistance. Everything turned into a blur after that preventing me from thinking straight. Not aware if Justin was dead or not, I remained frozen, my eyes never leaving his body.

"Ma'am, step aside. We need to get the victim inside," the male voice repeated.

"Lani! Lani," I heard my name as my co-worker KK shook me, "come inside so that we can figure out what the hell happened. I'm so tired of this bum ass stick 'em up fools!" she spat while escorting me inside.

Still, in a daze, all that replayed in my head was Justin's smile. Within a matter of minutes, the love of my life had been shot right before my eyes. It made no sense that it happened on hospital grounds and to the most amazing man I knew.

"Why? Why? Why?" I repeated to myself like a crazy woman pacing back and forth.

"Lani, we need to get some information from you. Try to calm down, honey. The doctors are doing everything they can to save him. Focus baby girl," she repeated.

"Okay. He's going to be alright," I recited taking deep breaths in and out.

"Is Justin allergic to any medications? Does he have a primary doctor that we can contact? Does he have any kinfolks?" KK bombarded me with what seemed like a hundred questions.

Once I answered her questions, she left me in the waiting room but promised to return as soon as possible. I took a seat, let my head fall inside the palms of my head, and prayed to the heavens for a miracle. The vibration from my pocket made me jump as if something crawled on me. Quickly retrieving my phone, I answered it.

"Hello."

"Where the fuck you at and are you okay?" were the first words Kofi Jr. spat into the phone.

"I'm still at the hospital. No, I'm not okay. Justin was shot and is in surgery right now," I managed to speak.

"What the fuck happened? Never mind, I'm on my way so don't move," he demanded, not evening say bye.

I tucked the phone back in my pocket and stood to my feet no longer able to sit still. I began to pace back and forth again when KK returned as promised only this time her somber expression revealed bad news.

"KK, please don't tell me he's—"

I couldn't even finish the sentence from the devastation. All I could do was breakdown as my body gave out, and I fell to the floor. KK got on the floor and did her best to console me by wrapping her arms around me like a mama bear.

"Aye, what's going on here?" I heard my cousin's voice grow closer and closer until he appeared in front of me.

"Justin was shot twice, and the doctor wasn't able to stop the bleeding. One of the bullets hit a main artery," KK described in detail.

The two eventually got me off the floor, outside and into Kofi Jr.'s car. During the ride, my head laid slumped over in the direction of the window as the objects from the outside swiftly passed by. Mute the entire time; my cousin never pushed me to say anything. He knew how upset and in shock I'd been.

Through the black and gold gate, we slowly drove under the driveway canopy on the east entrance of the mansion. The bright lights that surrounded the estate made me instantly squint my already puffy eyes. One of the bodyguards opened the door the second the car was put into park. Upon getting out, I slung my legs out and placed my left hand on the inside of the car for balance. That's when I glanced down at the ring on my finger prompting a tear to flow down my cheek.

"Lani, I know you are not trying to hear shit that I'm saying right now, but you are still young and will eventually meet another dude. Hopefully, we like his ass, but you can dream. Go to your wing and get cleaned up. I'm about to order a big ass pizza and some chicken wings from Pizza Hut. I'll check in when the food gets here," Kofi Jr. announced.

"Yup," I managed to say faintly.

I walked up the carpeted circular cherry wooden staircase and down the long hallway that led to my wing. Once inside my suite, I began to shed out of my clothing until my bare yellow ass was exposed to the cool-ness. Upon entering the white French doors of my master bathroom, my feet slapped against the beige, porcelain tile floor. I turned up the heat a few notches to get it toasty then walked into the oversized shower. The warm water streamed over me as I cleaned my body. The washcloth snagged on the ring, which brought about a fresh batch of tears.

I tried to wash away the pain and tears, but it didn't work. After-wards, I wrapped inside a large, light blue bath towel walking over to the vanity. One glance in the mirror horrified me. My eyes had grown puffy, and my hair was disheveled. A sista looked exactly how I felt—a hot ass mess. Unable to torture myself, I decided to remove the ring from my finger in the process. By the time that I dressed and picked up the dirty clothes from the floor, a knock at the door echoed.

"Excuse me, ma'am, but your delivery is here. I have a pan style pineapple and ham pizza, plain wings, and a fat ass blunt," the man's voice announced through the walkie-talkie.

I laughed and opened one of the double doors to find my crazy cousin standing and holding the food. He came inside and set up in the sitting area alcove where the fireplace and flat screen television were located. By that time, it was already three in the morning as we ate, smoked, and laughed at Dave Chappelle. Having company made all the difference when I smoked. Shit, I couldn't feel or think. Right before passing out, I remembered Jr. throwing a fleece blanket over me before he snuck out.

---

TWO WEEKS AFTER THE ORDEAL, my ass was still mentally messed up. All I did was smoke and pop antidepressant pills. My uncle had traveled to Jamaica on business leaving me under the protection of my cousins. Of course, Kofi Jr. checked in on me almost every five minutes in person and via FaceTime. During that most depressive phase in my life, memories of my parents' death resurfaced too. I vowed never to love again because that shit broke my heart into tiny pieces.

By the end of the month, my uncle demanded that I quit my job because he'd go apeshit if anything happened to me. He claimed that if I remained close to home, I'd be protected, which would ease his mind. Upset at his demand, I understood, but the shit was lame because that was my source of independence. In the meantime, my cousins continued to teach me the rules of the game to ensure that I was equipped with the street knowledge to survive.

## FOUR YEARS **LATER**

Hard to stay asleep, I laid in my queen-sized bed awaken by a bad dream. My tank top had grown cold and wet forcing me to get up. It had to be damn near one in the morning, not to mention quiet. I slung the sheet back, got up to change tops. Shaking from the central air that circulated through the room, it had my nipples rock hard. Dressed in a fresh t-shirt, I grabbed a Fiji water from my mini fridge, taking a few gulps to quench my thirst. To give my ass a break from the bed, I moved to the sitting area and turned on the flat screen that hung above the fireplace. I turned off the central air and cracked open a window hoping for a summer breeze. Earlier had been a scorcher with temperatures in the mid-80s.

I retrieved the RAW stash box from the ottoman and grabbed a pre-rolled joint the size of my finger. Everyone in the family smoked except KD, who was the eldest of the clan. He always claimed that it had to be one sober member with a clear head. Shit, not me. Marijuana had grown to be my aid instead of the pills the doctor prescribed for my depression and anxiety. Coping with the death of the three people who meant the world to me changed how I behaved and reacted to life. It was crazy how Justin appeared in my dreams almost every night causing me to relive his being killed in front of me. Between the dreams and depression, my uncle insisted I remained close to home. That meant having a cousin or escort accompany me whenever I left from the premise.

I texted Jr., only to find out he had left home. We were Virgos, so our bond was really like siblings. We got into trouble together, and he has even helped me sneak out a few times to see a boy. That boy happened to be Justin, the one who stole my heart and helped me get through the darkest times of my teenage years.

Matter a fact, Justin had been the only guy my uncle allowed me to have in our home. His suave gentleman persona and protective instincts for me pleased Uncle K. Justin showed respect at all times, even when I pressured him into taking my virginity. Justin and I had been vibing to some of the best songs of 2014 while we toked up. Teary-eyed at the mere thought of him made me quickly light up in hopes of getting rid of the sadness that consumed me. Needless to see my body felt the calming effects, yet my mind went in overdrive. A magical moment I'd never forget nor tell a soul took me back to that night we made love.

*It had been two months before he proposed, and most of my family was gone away on business except Jr. Although he checked in on us periodically, he went off to do his own thing but remained on the mansion grounds.*

*The lights were set in dim mode as we enjoyed each other's company as lovers did. The sounds of R&B 90s music softly played while he held me in his arms, which quickly escalated. As soon as he began to stroke my hair, a tingling sensation shot through my body, my nipples hardened, and the overwhelming warmth between my legs— all signs that I was ready to take the next step, and my body didn't want to wait.*

*"Are you sure you want to do this? I don't want you to feel pressured into pleasing me. Sex is only a portion of being in a relationship. We have time to do plenty of that," Justin admitted.*

*"This is what I want more now than ever. I'm ready Justin. It's you that I want to make me a woman," I confessed, staring deep into*

his enticing eyes. With my hormones raging and me being high, I yearned to have him touch me.

Justin leaned in to kiss me. When his lips pressed against mine, I closed my eyes to relish in the moment. His hands unbuttoned the white button down top exposing my breasts, which he anxiously squeezed and fondled. Becoming moist between the legs just from his touch made me wonder what the sex would be like and if I'd enjoy it. He pulled back to take a breather.

"Let's move to the bed where we can get more comfortable," he suggested. It was clear we were about to move into third base.

In motion towards the bed, I locked my door to ensure no one walked in on us. Justin stripped me naked and took it nice and slow as he kissed, sucked, and licked me all over. I occasionally jerked from his tongue as it tickled. When he gently pried open my legs, the rapid beat of my heart seemed as if it would pound out my chest. My legs started to slightly shake as I anticipated what was about to happen. With eyes shut tight, his warm tongue started to lap around my clit and vulva.

"Ahh... This feels so good," I moaned.

On my back, I gripped the sheets tightly in my hands as shit got more intense. Unsure how he learned what he was doing to me, I wish I could give the bitch a high five for the great job he did. Although it was my first time receiving head, I was sure there wasn't another nigga who could do it like Justin. Just as the warm juices flowed from my pussy, I felt a pinch followed by slight pressure.

"Damn baby my shit eased in smooth, you weren't lying when you said you were ready. If I hurt you tap my back and I'll stop," he instructed.

In a slow thrusting motion, I eventually grew comfort having his thick base inside me. My first time had me on cloud nine, Justin was the only man I needed and wanted. We had officially shared our minds and bodies, a new stepping-stone towards spouse hood.

# THREE
## LANI KINGSTON

Groggy and not ready to get up yet, I rolled over to grab the walkie-talkie and yelled that I wasn't ready to eat breakfast. When my head plopped down on the pillow, my eyelids drooped closed, but the sound of rapping on my door made my head spring up.

"WHAT? IT'S OPEN!" I yelled out wondering who was on the other side.

"Wake yo azz up, my nigga!" Kaine spat on his way in with a wooden tray.

"Man, I'm so tired. It's those damn pills," I confessed in motion to sit up.

"Here goes breakfast. It's some French toast, eggs, bacon, and assorted fruits. Eat and get washed up because today is the day that you learn another piece of the puzzle," Kaine warned me before making his way out the suite.

The smile I wore slowly diminished as my stomach growls went into overdrive. I drizzled syrup across the cinnamon coated bread and went to town. The eggs were fluffy and cheesy just how I liked them. Each fork full tasted so damn good. I saved the fruit for last not leaving anything behind. Satisfied with the most important meal of the day, I sat the tray aside and laid back down for a few minutes. I knew it was only a matter of time before one of my cousins' bust through the door to make sure my ass was physically awake and out the bed. Instead, they took turns being jackasses playing with the walkie-talkies until I finally turned the covers loose.

"Alexa, play Kevin Gates," I loudly spoke as I climbed out the bed and then quickly made the bed up, smoothing the comforter.

Within forty minutes, I showered, dressed, and put my hair in a ponytail to the back. On the way out the door, I retrieved the food tray and made the trip to the kitchen. From there, I headed down the tile floor stairs to the place we spent ninety percent of the time. The Situation Room, as my uncle called it, was used for family debriefings and personal meetings he had with those he trusted.

"Morning everybody," I greeted as I waved my hand in the air and took a seat next to my fav. He was caking on the phone with some Trollip who had sent him some personal pictures.

"Dang, get out my phone, nosy," he blurted then turned the screen face down and placed it on the table.

"My bad, it was right there in my peripheral view," I explained followed by a laugh he hated.

Once Kaden and Kaine entered the room and took their seats, my uncle cleared his throat. It was his way of demanding our eyes upfront, no bullshit. We had to pay close attention. I sat up straight with an almost perfect posture and watched the big body man with a husky voice speak.

"Alright, let's get down to the business so that we can be on our way. One of our boys got caught up. He got arrested on his way to Chicago. On standby, we can still operate like normal," he explained.

"Does this impact us hard or lightly?" Kofi Jr. questioned.

"It's not a direct impact, but we can't take any chances, so the next batch we prep for distro needs to be skimmed a little. A drought is coming so we need to stack that paper," Uncle Kingston answered back.

"Do you think old dude is gonna snitch, or if somebody snitched on him? That could be bad for business on our behalf if our name surfaces," Kaine inquired.

"I've thought about that as well, and my people are on it. I should know something this evening from an old friend," Uncle K assured him but addressed us all.

He clasped his hands and placed them on his belly, then leaned back in the black leather high back chair. He opened the floor up for those who had noteworthy shit to share. Silent, I just observed and took mental notes while the guys took turns speaking up.

"Pops, word on the street is that Lenny's dropped off the grid, but his ass still in the city somewhere.. I'm sure he has heard it too. My corner boys got their ears and eyes open ready to report anything they see going down," Kaden add his two cents.

"What now?" I asked the same question everybody wanted an answer to but bit their tongue.

"I plan to call a brief sit down at one of our secure locations to assure the partners our main connection to the supply won't dry up. Lani, it's time to sharpen those skills. I need you to be at your best," his stern voice spoke to me.

"Yes sir," I answered without saying another word.

"Be sharp and accurate because lives are depended on it," he orders as his words gave me the chills.

"Yes sir," I respectfully answered.

"You'll get updates in twenty-four hours on the next move. If there is nothing else, Jr. and Kaine, I need y'all to go collect. You know what to do if you run into any problems," he asked rhetorically.

"Yes sir," they both answered seconds apart from one another. Everyone had removed themselves from the table leaving the two of us.

"Lani, we have a few things to chat about before you leave. First, I want to know how you've been. Please be honest," he encouraged.

"I still have bad dreams here and there, but the doctor said that would happen. Being here all day doesn't help," I spoke truthfully, not trying to be ungrateful.

"You and your cousins are my soft spot. Niggas know I'd die or go to war for y'all. I know you're a young adult, but your last name is the consequence of being born a Kingston. It's just the way the game works."

"Yes, that is clear, but it sucks," I hissed.

"You got it made, niece. Your father and I have bounced around from house to house because our parents traveled trafficking drugs. I knew as the years went by that their absence was permanent. We had to be tough, hustle, and feed ourselves."

"Wow, I didn't know all that uncle.

---

UNCLE KINGSTON MADE it very clear his expectations of me, so I made sure to remain sharp and sober. I made sure not to smoke or take my meds in an effort to be effective. By the time he had summoned all of the key players to the sit-down, I felt ready to complete the mission. On that day instead of rolling with Kofi Jr., my uncle suggested that we ride together, something we rarely did. When we both got inside the black Denali, his attention had been glued to his phone until the driver began to drive away.

"Niece, there will be four men arriving this morning. Each man brings something to the table and makes me lots of money. However, it has come to my attention that they can't be trusted anymore. Before I make any hasty decisions, I need you to do your thing. Just watch their behavior and report directly to me afterwards."

"You got it. What if your information is false?"

"Let me worry about that dear."

"How do you do it every day? This life ain't no joke," I questioned. The flashback entered my mind from the first time that I witnessed my uncle commits murder.

"Survival instincts. When you grow up around certain environments, things tend to resonate. In this game, I gotta always watch my back, never letting my guard down. It's always niggas out to get me, so my motivation every day is money, my family, and leaving a legacy."

Before I could speak, his phone went off, and he diverted his full attention to the screen. Unsure what it was that caused him to let out a deep sigh, he then yelled "*Shit!*" before making a call.

"Aye K-Murder, we got a visitor in town on behalf of Lenny, the snake. You know what to do. We'll discuss later. One," he expressed.

"Alright Lady K, let's do this niece!"

At our destination Uncle K didn't bother to wait for his driver to open his car door, something I felt was too dangerous for a man of his status. We exited the black truck and strolled step by step, like bosses. I felt like a mini-boss as I was dressed in a navy blue Anne Klein pantsuit. My hair was slicked to the back in a neat bun. Wester Tires Warehouse had been a secret spot only known by family and those who were given the location. Inside was a closed-off space in the back that had recently been turned into a soundproof meeting room.

Within a matter of minutes, several men entered a few at a time until the seats were filled. Alongside my Uncle Kingston, all the training had paid off, and I was at the table with the big boys. Uncle Kingston. Not threatened by the many sets of eyes glued on me, my ears stood wide open as I gave the deep cold stare in return.

"I called you gentlemen here to discuss a few updates on the distro and a potential problem we all need to keep an eye and ear open to. One of the main connects ran into an unfortunate law situation. That leaves us all in a bind, which means that we need to do some price negotiations. This has sent a ripple effect to the other connections who have shut down their operations." The baritone voice held the attention of each man, including myself.

Upright with a perfect posture, I eyeballed each man welcoming eye contact. In class, I learned that eyes don't lie. Those who couldn't hold a gaze tended to have something to hide. Most divert after a few seconds but not me. I loved to search deep into the pupils of those who withheld the truth.

"So, what do you propose we do in the meantime?" a bearded,

caramel skin tone man sat forward asked and sat forward. He placed his hand to his face, rubbed his beard, and waited for Uncle K to answer.

"Up your prices, find a new connect, or step on that shit a little more. I can't reassure you when operations will resume. However, there is a possible option I'm currently exploring. Let's move on to the next line of business." The tone of his voice changed along with his demeanor, which was my cue to watch each man like a hawk for any signs of guilt.

Three men immediately shifted in their seats, which either meant they ass had grown numb from sitting or their guilty conscious got to them. Their body language warranted more attention because I was unsure of their guilt. Despite the uncertainty, it didn't stop Uncle from K from chewing niggas out.

"No disrespect to you or yours, but how do we know that nigga is not snitching on us right now? We are all vulnerable right now, which jeopardizes our operations!" another voice yelled out.

"I hear you, and I understand your uncertainty right now. However, as I just stated I'm exploring another option. Starting today make sure the street crews understand that there are absolutely no freebies."

All eyes and ears, I watched and listened to everything Uncle K said and did. He commanded a room and had grown ass men scared to speak their mind at times. As a pupil of the game, I focused on the teacher as a way to master his techniques. Sometimes I knew that was his reason for having me assist in such sit-downs. When it was all said and done my gut proved right, the three men lost their lives as a result of not showing loyalty. Afterwards, we went home while Uncle K resumed business per usual.

# FOUR
# LENOX SCOTT

Some folks called me a hoodlum. Others say I'm a thug, but I'm just a nigga from the hood who made shit happen. Despite my business preference to slang dope, I tried to be a good dude. I never took shit from anybody. Instead, I hustled every day, which was the motto that I lived by. Growing up, my father taught me street shit the average thirteen-year-old shouldn't have known until adulthood.

The family had been plagued with crime and violence going back to my great, great, granddaddy who was a slave. According to family history, he reached his breaking point and killed as many white folks, including his master. It had been his revenge for the mistreatment of his black people who suffered from beatings. Able to escape with only a flesh wound, he managed to join the many that traveled through the Underground Railroad in search for freedom. Eventually, he settled on the Southside of Chicago where he died in 1962.

My grandfather passed away in 2002 and took all of his secrets to the grave. It was rumored he had a connection that was directly linked to the mob. Next was my Uncle Keith who was known as a stick-up kid. He hooked up with the wrong crew and began to rob banks, which turned out to be lucrative until they got greedy.

According to my father, a job went wrong and resulted in five people getting shot dead. All four men were caught and sent to Alcatraz Federal Penitentiary. Not a soul ratted the other one out until the day they died, which surprising happened within weeks of each other. Of course, as time passed drugs became an epidemic, which is where my father's street activities came into play.

Lastly, was my Aunt Ruthie who moved from Milwaukee to a little college town located in Blackwater, Wisconsin. She tended to do things differently from the others contributing to her longevity and wealth. Instead of staying in the hood, she moved away to get a peace of mind while she distributed pure cocaine around the region. Her known occupation as a farmer allowed her to portray the older woman persona as she made more money than the stores she supplied dairy products to. Although she offered me to join her empire, I respectfully declined not wanting any part of that life. Surprisingly she accepted my choice, but wouldn't accept my decline to move nearby. Eventually, I moved to Blackwater as well just in the opposite direction.

The cycle should've been broken with me in the 1980s, yet the generational curse continued. I learned how to cook dope, cut it, bag it, and sell that shit. Although I became a street thug and dealer, I took my ass to school every day no matter what. Education had been something nobody could take away from me. My father didn't knock me either. Life in the teen years grew more complicated as my father expected more from me. His pressure unleashed my rage that I in return took out on them fools in the streets.

Each night I laid in bed unable to sleep from the loud thud sounds that came from the radiator in my room. Beyond annoyed there wasn't shit I could do but dream for a better life. I knew one day that I'd have enough money to live in a place that was better than the box of an apartment. My environment became motivation to hustle hard until I could change the way we lived. Growing up in my hood, we made money at a young age, and that shit felt good as hell. The niggas on the block that I used to see slanging and banging were like family more, specifically older brothers or role models. The street life turned me into a child hustler and young killa. I used to be quick to shoot a nigga without blinking twice. However that shoot em shit got old.

After high school graduation, I grew more mature with a sense of the business skill set, in exchange my hotheaded days ceased, and a sophisticated hoodlum emerged. Unable to attend the college of my choice, I took two classes per semester at UWM. Eventually, I earned my degree in Marketing but didn't limit myself from learning a little about Criminal Justice. I taught my pops what I learned, to ensure that we always kept money accessible.

Over the years life changed, and I matured. The streets didn't do shit but leave fools dead from gunshots to the body or locked in a closet for a cell. As a black street yet educated man, I started a small insurance company. At first, it felt as if I had sold out, but I realized it was growth and knowledge that made me change my ways.

IT HAD BEEN ALMOST two years since I'd set foot back home or saw my father. We had put a distance between us due to my decision to go a legal route in life. Although he claimed to be proud, his actions spoke otherwise. Out of respect, I checked up on him periodically since he was still my father, but the bond had changed. Imagine my surprise when I got a call from him, which didn't turn out to be a social call either. In a good mood, I answered without thinking twice.

"What's up, pops? How are you living?"

"Hey, son. I'm living shit. I could use your help though." He wasted no time asking for a favor.

"How so?" I interrogated.

"I can't go into details right now. Pay your old man a visit sooner than later. I could really use some advice," he hinted. The sound of his voice indicated something wasn't right.

"Let me move some stuff around on my calendar, and I'll be to visit before the end of the week."

"Good to hear. Make sure to bring your girls. It might get wild," he warned.

"C'mon pops, it's like that. I'll see you tomorrow night," I confirmed now that I had more knowledge about the situation.

"I can always rely on you to have my back. See you when you arrive. Be safe, son. One love," he said before the call ended.

"FUCK!" I yelled out of frustration as I laid the phone down on the desk.

When my pops said bring your girls, he referred to my pistols that never left my side. That was a clear sign he had drama in the streets and needed me. In contemplation of my next moves, I lit a blunt to help me think.

Cruising through the streets that exposed me to violence, I was known as the little smooth light skin nigga on Burleigh, Center, Auer, Locust, and North Avenue. I never fucked with the east side or the niggas because of the long-term feud. Live by the gun, die by the gun was the street and drug game rule that they lived by.

My pops relocated to a quiet neighborhood. He lived off in seclusion in a spot where niggas wouldn't dare search for him. A long-term member of the streets, his age had caught up to him, and his reign in the streets didn't mean much anymore. New crews, dealers, and connections had changed how the streets were running and by whom.

I pulled in the driveway, took a deep breath, and exited the vehicle. The shadow darted swiftly past the window followed by the sound of the locks on the door.

"I'm here, pops!" I made sure to announce myself carefully not to catch an accidental bullet.

The door opened a little more giving me a visual of the salt and pepper goatee man who resembled David Banner.

"Son, welcome home," he said, embracing me with a tight hug.

"I like what you've done with the place. How long you plan on staying here?"

"I'm not moving anymore son. This is it right here. I'll die in this home," he commented and sat back down in his La-Z-Boy recliner.

"Pops, please tell me what the hell is going on around here? I need some answers before I get wrapped back up in this mess."

"Damn nigga, you cut to the chase," was his response as he sat up in his chair. "Same shit different day. My corner, his corner, territory shit. The corners have been filled with these disrespect ass kids who think they're Scarface because they are moving a little weight."

"This generation is beyond wild, but what does that have to do with you?"

"I refused to a young punk disrespect me now it's a bunch of bull-shit popping off from other leaders connected to them. Look, we can discuss everything in detail tomorrow, tonight it's just father and son time," he hinted for me to shy away from the topic.

"I guess, but don't bullshit me," I warned. The rest of the night, we drank beer and chopped it up about the good old days.

---

THE NEXT MORNING, I felt refreshed as fuck from a good night rest on the Serta memory foam mattress. My dad kept a bedroom for me in the event that I needed a place to stay or had to move in a care-taker. Despite only getting five hours of sleep, a nigga was so well rested that I got out of bed and made breakfast for the old man and me. We needed some bonding time, not to mention a plan on how to handle his problem.

After searching in the fridge, I found bologna, mustard, eggs, and a few potatoes and did what I did best. I hooked some shit up and made a meal out of nothing. We enjoyed a fried bologna and egg sandwich with cut up potatoes on the side. The bologna had been fried perfectly with the ring crispy drizzled with mustard.

"Alright pops, we need to chat. Lay out the facts and don't leave out nothing."

"Look son take a seat. This situation is bigger than you think and may require you to stay longer than I admitted over the phone," he confessed, not breaking eye contact.

"I should've known," I mumbled and took a seat. "My ears are opened.

"Shit has changed since back in the day. Young niggas don't know the meaning of respect. I'm supposed to be out of the game but have been doing business on my own. This means not hitting anybody hand but mine. About a month ago, a personal deal got back to one of the plugs.

"I knew it was more to the damn story. Keep going," I demanded.

"I refused to pay extra to the Center Street Crew. The lead nigga tried to intimidate me. As a result, I chopped that fool's hand off. Word got back to the main supplier, who happened to be the uncle of the boy."

"People looking for you and your stash on the low?" I questioned.

"That's the gist of it. Niggas can't eat on account of my actions."

"Shiiit, you chopped a nigga's hand off, pops. He's not a regular dude. He is related to the supplier. This is all bad, but I'm rockin' wit ya no matter what."

"Shit will work out. In the meantime, my old ass needs a nap.

"You right pops," I agreed. "Shit, after I smoke, a nap is in my future too."

---

I WAS ONLY SUPPOSED to be in town for a week, but shit was more serious than I thought. My father had pissed a lot of folks off, so of course, he called me to help clean up his mess. Although he was my pops and I'd do anything for him, I had changed the way I moved and grew legit with clean hands. I guess the family curse found a way to lure me back despite my resistance.

A complex relationship could be a way to describe us. My loyalty had gone so far that I followed in his footsteps. I knew he loved me without a doubt, but when I revealed that it had been time for me to make my own footsteps I read something that indicated one's first child went through everything with them. I'd finally gotten out the game but then fell susceptible to sins of a father. That shit was so real.

# FIVE

# LANI KINGSTON

The downside to being a Kingston was the notion that I couldn't do shit without them in my business. Uncle K ordered Jr. to chaperone me outside the home ever since the random incident that killed Justin. To this day, we never found out who the two men were or what their motive was because nothing was taken. I understood my need to be safe, but as a young woman in need of freedom, I felt smothered.

"Aye big head, pops is about to call a sit-down, so get yo butt to the Situation Room. Oh, you might want to change too because you smell like that bag," Keon warned.

"Alright, let me change quickly. I'll be right down. Thanks, cuz," I said and blew him a kiss before closing the door.

I changed into a gray Adidas jogging suit and took the dreaded route down to the room where everyone waited. Serious about each meeting, my uncle would have a mini notepad and pen on the table in of our spots.

After we were dismissed, I lingered around to speak in private the things I needed to get off my chest. As the leader and head of all decisions, I knew it was all or nothing to pitch my idea of opening up a clothing store.

"Uncle, I need to chat with you about an idea that I've been thinking about and I hope to get your blessing on it. To make a long story short, I want to open my own clothing store and sell cute and affordable stuff for women," I tried to sound convincing.

"Tell me more," his baritone voice announced as he took a seat and leaned back in the chair.

"Well I'm trying to move forward with life, and you know fashion is my thing. I need to keep occupied. Otherwise, I'll go stir crazy in this palace. I'm beginning to feel like a prisoner in my own home," I admitted truthfully. "You know what else. You could use the store to clean money as you do at the barbershop," I added.

My eyes watched his facial expressions as he thought about my proposal, not saying a word. I grew nervous he'd shut down my idea, but surprisingly, he agreed to give me a chance to prove myself. Lately, he had a real soft spot for me and didn't realize the anniversary of my parents' death approached. It shocked me that sixteen years had already passed since the horrific ordeal.

Sundays were the time we gathered for a briefing, evening dinner to talk life, but most importantly, it was a tradition to sip Hennessy and watch *Game of Thrones*. Quality time was one of the only things I looked forward to once a week. The fellas had a bomb ass home theater with a wet bar in the basement. Upon entering, there were eight leather seats with padded headrests. The cup holders were lighted with an ambient blue along with the floor and under the seats. It was way better than spending money or being bothered with annoying moviegoers.

Uncle K had been very strict on engaging with outsiders just because of his profession, not to mention those who wanted to kill him or any member of his family. Therefore, we made sure to have fun together whenever possible. When I was a small child, we used to do the same thing. Those used to be the good old days.

# SIX

# KINGSTON JR

Every morning when my eyes opened, I thanked the man upstairs for letting me see another day. Despite my actions and wrongs, it was a firm belief of mine that there was a higher power. A humble person, my lifestyle was a dangerous one that could claim my life at any time. Therefore, I did my best to keep cool without putting a bullet in somebody's head. In my family, you couldn't be soft or scared to pop a fool if necessary. Shit, I popped niggas for looking at me wrong. Known as the hot head of the bunch from an early age, my father always said he knew I'd grow up to be a killa. So much so that he decided to give me his name although I was the third son. Most fathers name their firstborn son Jr. but not my pops. He was different.

My mother, rest her soul, never argued or interfered when it came to my pops raising us. She never approved of her babies being involved with drugs or the street life. However, all she could do was be the best mother despite it all. A daughter of the drug game herself, she knew not to ask questions but to play her role.

The first time I took a life, I was only thirteen. From that point on, I grew up to be a gangsta. When I watched movies like *The Godfather*, *New Jack City*, and *Sugar Hill*, my fascination with street life deemed my father to name me after him. My reckless behavior typically caused trouble, but I learned trust was something that could get you dead that's why I only trusted my brothers. In the dope game, one thing was for sure— enemies came a dime a dozen. Fools on all sides of town in Milwaukee knew not to try anything stupid with any member of our crew.

Like father like son, I loved money and women, but family always came first. I am my brothers' keeper, and that included my cousin Lani. She lived with us damn near her entire life and was little sister we never had. My father took her in once her parents were killed. The love for money and power was the cause of their demise.

Nevertheless, we killed the niggas responsible. The death of my aunt and uncle deemed to painful for my mom. She ended up committing suicide, and to this day, no one ever knew why she did it other than speculation of guilt.

My mom and Lani's mom were sisters. My mom was the one who introduced my aunt to Uncle Devon. He had been a part of the family for so long that he witnessed the births of my brothers and I. Eventually when he met Aunt Kim, he fell head over heels in love, and the story is history. Apparently they got involved in the family business following in my father's footsteps. Years went by, and we lived in luxury until small changes began to occur. It was rumored that Lani's parents got greedy and in too deep. One story claimed they stole dope and tried to pull a fast one on the notorious hood nigga Black. Another insisted it was all set up and was a power move against my pops. We tried to shield Lani from the lies, but I eventually told her the truth once she reached an age where she understood.

Lani and I were like the male and female version of each other. The shit was kind of scary at times. I took on the responsibility to protect her from Raggedy Ann type bitches and dudes who saw a pretty face. It became my duty and role to be her big brother and protector. In the process, it also taught me to be more mindful of how I treated females.

"AYE JR., go round everybody up and have them come to the Situation Room for a discussion," Kaden ordered.

"Aight, but you could just radio everybody. Shit this place too big, nigga."

"Yo lazy ass needs the workout! Stop smoking all them damn blunts, and you will be cool," he clowned me.

"Fuck you nigga!" I spat then laughed.

"We are waiting for KD to get here anyway, so you got time G. Oh, and tell Lani to please cover herself. I'm not trying to get cussed out."

"Pops must be coming too if you are talking like that."

"He might. KD wasn't sure though, so let's be ready." Kaden was my older brother, so despite giving him shit, I did what he told me.

"Alright, I'll be right back."

I left from the kitchen and went up the back stairs that lead to the different wings of the mansion headed for Lani's area. I knocked three times on her door before she snatched it opened. She disappeared into the bathroom while jamming to Lil Wayne.

"Be down in the meeting spot in ten minutes. Pops and KD are on the way."

"Oh shit, let me get dressed then because I'm not trying to get cussed out. I'll be down in a minute," she stated still dancing to the music.

"Don't take all day, please," I said then closed her door back.

I walked down the long hallway until it curved to a narrow stairwell. That stairwell led right into the Gold Room also known as the ganja spot. We lived in a luxurious mansion with a beautiful view of the lake and park. The four-story nine-bedroom palace was made for the kings that we were. My family was untouchable, paid, and destined to run shit.

As soon as I approached the two marble stairs, I ran right into my pops and KD coming down the stairwell from the left of me. Both were dressed so clean that they looked and smelled like money.

"Damn bro, you look like a million bucks," I gave him a hand-shake followed by a hug. Turning my attention to my father, I voiced, "Pops, it's good to see you. How was the flight?" We embraced and proceeded to the room until the rest of the family joined us.

"Aye son, while we wait, let me holla at you for a minute," he pulled me to the side.

"How is your cousin doing with the store thing? She has been taking her meds?" he questioned.

"She's good. She's still excited and glad to get out the house keeping busy doing what she likes to do. Trust me. She's been chill except for her normal self when she doesn't want to do what she's told."

"Good, that's settled. Let's get to the table," he ordered as we strolled to join the crew.

The eight of us took a seat around the cherry wood table in the white cushioned chairs trimmed in wood like a scene in a mob flick. My father and KD sat at the head of the table, while the rest of us took the closest seat.

The moment my pops started talking my phone began to vibrate, but my attention never left from the front of the room. I finally glanced at the screen to see Teresa's name. That trick thought we were a couple because we fucked a few times. Although her pussy was good, she blew my phone up, not to mention tried to stick to a nigga like glue. I made a mental note to block her digits after the meeting. Fuck 'em and block was my motto. I know, my ass ain't shit, but I'm cool with that.

"Your brother and I have some good and bad news, but it won't affect us making money. We lost a few workers, and a big-time supplier got busted. Although other suppliers are skeptical, a few are willing to business with us. Our white boy Dave put a bug in my ear about a trustworthy new connection. KD, explain it while I take this call," my father requested as he stepped out the room quickly.

"Okay, pops want Lani and Jr. to travel to Blackwater, Wisconsin to meet a woman known as Aunt Ruthie. According to Dave and another source, she is big-time and looks like the average older woman. It would only be for a day no more than two. Feel her out get a vibe and check shit out. Don't say nothing unnecessary or make any kind of deals just in case that bitch a nark."

"Why do I have to go?" Lani questioned. She should have known by now that this wasn't an option but an order.

"Lay, you are going because it is required of you and because you have a role to play like everybody. If you have a problem, talk to pops when he returns. Oh, and you can kiss that store goodbye," his words jabbed.

"I'm cool. I'm just saying sometimes it would be nice to be asked instead of ordered," she voiced in a more respectful tone.

There was a brief silence before KD continued with his words and then my father returned and took his seat. I didn't have any questions because I was down for whatever. KD continued with details for the travel to Blackwater. Out of the corner of my eye, I noticed Lani's pouted lips, so I gave her a little kick under the table. She kicked the shit out of me back then smiled. Pops made the last remarks then dismissed us to be free.

"Cuz you should take me to the mall or somewhere outside of this place," Lani hovered over me with a smile.

"I gotta run errands anyway, come on, let's roll out," I replied, surprising her.

---

I PREPPED for the trip with Lani packing extra changing clothes for a day or two to handle shit then get back to the Mil. My pops always had a deal in the works to benefit the family, which is another reason that I never asked questions. Full of lasagna, garlic bread, and salad a nigga was ready to smoke a blunt. Pops had the chef prepare our favorite meal before hitting the road. Before walking out the side entrance of the mansion, my father stopped Lani and I. He said a travel prayer to bless our route with my brothers surrounding us.

"Y'all know what to do and how to do it. Be safe and always watch each other's back. Lani, baby girl, try not to entice or hurt anyone. We know how quick you are to snap out or blurt shit. Kill only in self-defense. We don't need trouble during this deal."

"Relax, Unc. I'll be cool the entire time. I know my role. My meds are in my purse, besides the ladies' man over here is the one who causes the drama."

"It ain't my fault that a nigga is handsome and wealthy." Everybody cracked a laugh then Kaine disappeared.

Right before Lani and I headed towards the truck, Kaine caught up to us with a box in hand. With a raised eyebrow, I watched as he handed it to her to open. Suspicious, when she raised the lid, we all yelled in unison "Hell naw." Kaine fool ass got her a pink baby Glock. Her eyes lit up in awe of the gift.

"I love it thank you, K! This bitch is hot! Oh, sorry Uncle K," she apologized while she continued to admire her new toy. Her excitement made me proud, yet it terrified me at the same time. Not trigger happy; she just had anger issues like all of us.

"Hell yeah, it's time you had your own personalized piece since your part of the clan."

Pops leaned to the side staring at my brother then shook his head before he busted out in laughter. He knew it was a waste of breath to even address Kaine. I laughed too because you couldn't fix someone stuck in their ways.

"Alright hit us the minute y'all make it. One love," Kaine and KD expressed.

Lani and I tossed our bags in the back of the Denali. Close to six o'clock, we got on the road in an effort to avoid the work traffic. Ready to roll, I hit the gas. Lani played DJ and lit the blunt once we hit the highway. My cuz was such a down ass chick that we enjoyed the vibe together. Like a sister, her ass was forbidden to do certain shit, but the rebel that she was she snuck and did shit smoothly.

# SEVEN

# LANI KINGSTON

In the front seat buzzed and still excited to receive my personalized gun, I finally felt like an official member of the business. For eleven years, I've undergone a mental and physical test by six different men who displayed six different personalities. Having a gun hadn't been a thought for me if it wasn't needed.

Upon entering nowhere land, we passed so many corn fields, farms, big ass cows and horses. It looked creepy as hell because all the roads looked the same once it started to get dark. Almost five minutes from the city, I grew less anxious when I spotted a Walmart across from the Baymont Inn & Suites. We parked the truck, snatched our bags, and headed inside to check into our rooms. The blond chick at the desk had been sitting but sprung to her feet the second we entered. She plastered a big grin on her face ready to greet us, but I think Becky liked chocolate.

"Good evening! Welcome to the Baymont Inn & Suites, I'm Melissa," she introduced herself. That tramp had a death stare on Kofi Jr so much so that I had to interrupt.

"Um, Melissa, can we speed up the process, please. I need to step to the lady's room."

"Oh yes, I'm sorry. There is actually one located around the corner," she pointed.

"Thanks. I'll be right back," I dropped my bag to the floor and disappeared around the corner. By the time I'd finished, Kofi Jr. had hit the corner carrying both our bags. There were only two floors to the establishment; my room was at the other end of the first floor.

I inserted the plastic key card into the door and waited until the light turned green then pushed it open. Upon stepping inside, the queen-sized bed appeared to look decent. I pulled the covers back, layer by layer, to check for bed bugs. It was a habit to examine the bed before just flopping inside them covers. With no bugs in sight, I proceeded to examine the rest of the room but was interrupted when Kofi knocked on the joining door. We made a quick Walmart run for some snacks, something to drink, and to survey the country town.

---

THAT NEXT MORNING Kofi Jr. hit my phone with the time that I needed to have my ass outside by the truck. Not a minute late, I opened the passenger door and slid in the seat ready to get business over. With the truck already started, Kofi Jr. had his phone out on speaker as the sound of the phone rang on the other end. On the second ring, Uncle K answered as if he had been waiting for the call.

"Sup pops. I got you on speaker, Lani sitting here too."

"Is everything straight?"

"Yes," both of us answered properly.

"I sent you the address of Grandma Ruthie house with a picture too. She surrounded by her farmland, animals, and snow," he coded in reference to cocaine.

In the passenger seat, I listened and watched with precision as we sat in the hotel parking lot. Jr. whipped out the second phone to review the address to where we had to drive for the meet and greet.

"Got it," he called out over the speaker.

"Use your judgment when you converse and watch ya surroundings at all times. Lady K, rely on your gut and woman's intuition. Don't let that nice old lady persona cloud your reading. Understand?"

"Yes uncle," I quickly replied. Whenever he called me Lady K, he expected me to perform and execute my task as he did with the guys.

"Jr. be cordial, you know the charming Kingston, but don't let grandma play you like a fiddle. Code language only, and hit me if shit goes sideways."

"Aiight pops, we'll check in afterwards. Love," my cousin noted.

He typed the address into the GPS, turned on the music, and drove out the lot. The brief drive through the city and downtown area reminded me of *The Andy Griffith Show* and their town Mayberry. The route led us to the back roads where the faint smell of cow shit hit my nostrils. I thought the ride would never end until the female computerized voice announced we'd reached our destination. In amazement, the Victorian style home and amount of land surrounding it had me sit up attentively.

"Damn, that's beautiful. This old lady is living nicely in the middle of nowhere," I commented while Jr. cautiously pulled into the long gravel driveway until we noticed her wave a hand. While he parked, I immediately surveyed the woman who stood and blew out smoke from what appeared to be a cigarette. When we exited the truck, an instant whiff of weed hit me quickly. Instantly she scored a point in my book, but the true test started the second she introduced herself.

"Morning. Y'all must be my expected guests on account of Dave," she greeted in a welcoming manner.

"Morning," Jr. spoke first then me.

Face to face with the attractive mocha-skinned woman sent off positive vibes. Appearance wise it was true to not judge a book by its cover because nothing about her screamed drug supplier. It's possible her natural gray hair aided her criminal occupation. I'd never met a female of her status who looked so normal. To keep from appearing like a statue, I finally opened my mouth.

"Ma'am, you have an amazing home. I've never seen anything this elegant. These types of homes are special," I expressed.

"Come, let's get inside. I'll give you a tour while we handle business. Only under two conditions," she stated. Jr. and I glanced at each other hoping that she wasn't on some bullshit.

"Take your shoes off upon entering, and don't call me ma'am. Everyone calls me Aunt Ruthie.

I let out a light sigh before plastering a smile as I nodded in agreement followed by a verbal answer, "Got it."

She led us into the side entrance where we slide out of our shoes then proceeded into the main portion of the house. We stood in the wood floor gourmet kitchen that took my breath away with the wood and granite counter tops. In the future, I dreamed of a home similar because of space. Aunt Ruthie started the tour from the second floor all the way through the fourth floor. Each room was dust free with each item in its place. It almost felt like a tour of a famous house. After the tour, we ended up back in the kitchen where we sat at the marble round table to discuss the reason for our visit.

"During my chat with Dave, he spoke highly of your uncle and the way he operated a business. I was pleased to hear how discrete and professional he is. That's my number one rule. So I'm willing to do a test trial."

"Aunt Ruthie, we are grateful for your willingness for a seat at the table. We understand you're a busy woman supplying the town with dairy products. I'm sure the eggs we ate for breakfast came from the farm. If you don't mind, how will the test trail work?" Jr. inquired.

I observed the healthy looking sixty-year-old white woman not able to comprehend how well she hid her truth. She looked like your typical grandma who smoked and enjoyed gardening. In the process of listening to the conversation, my eyes shifted back and forth between my cousin as he talked and the way she paused before answering questions. Nothing about her provoked red flags or signs of deception. If anything, her semi flirtatious stares proved that white women loved black men.

Unsure of her story, or how she got involved with drugs, I wanted to ask her a trillion questions both out of curiosity and just to be nosey. During our time at the table, I also wondered why she lived alone, how she managed to fool folks, and what would happen to her home if something happened to her.

As soon as we were inside the truck, Jr. backed out the driveway and waited until we drove a few miles from her location to hit up my uncle. Again, we had the speakerphone on during the update not going into specific details.

Before heading back to the hotel, we agreed on grabbing food, so we stopped at Culver's and went inside to eat. During that time, we chatted about our trip and what we assumed would happen with the deal between our uncle and Aunt Ruthie. I smashed my single bacon deluxe sandwich and fries then instantly grew sleepy between the short walk from the restaurant to the truck. When we returned to the hotel Jr. parked in a different location so that he could roll up before we went inside. Full and high, we headed to the room for a much-needed hour nap before hitting the road back to Milwaukee.

# EIGHT

# LANI KINGSTON

Beyond excited to view the store space that my uncle purchased, I played music while I applied a coat of Rose Fondu matte, liquid lipstick. My plump lips were natural and beautiful; the type hundreds of women spent money monthly to get.

*"You have ten minutes to bring yo ass down to the vehicle! Don't make us leave you!"* Kaine spat into the walkie-talkie.

*"Damn, I'm on my way give me a freaking break. This big ass maze of a home can take a minute. Don't leave me chump. Over."*

I took one last glance at myself to make sure the world was ready for me to grace them with my beauty. Quickly, I clipped my black leather Gucci fanny pack around my waist and jetted out of my suite. Just as suspected Kofi Jr. was behind the wheel and Kaine stood in irritation as I took my time exiting the east side entrance.

"Ms. Pritzy, get yo ass in the truck. I swear you gonna get some dude fucked up today," Kaine remarked as he shut the door behind me.

"Y'all know I gotta look good at all times before coming out in public. In case ya forgot, my outside activities had been limited. Thank you," I sarcastically said, causing Kaine to glance back.

"Lani, you do take forever to get ready, admit it cuz. It's all good though because you can't be busted hanging around me. Aye, changing topics right fast. Did pops explain in detail how the store will run?" Kaine questioned.

"He explained the basics and said he'd sit down with me again. Either way, I'm ready for the task. I'm almost twenty-four. I'm too old to be stuck at home while y'all have all the fun."

"Cuz, this business ain't no joke. Make sure you hear shit loud and clear whenever you are told to do something. You are a Kingston, an automatic target to our enemies. Always keep ya eyes and ear open, and don't trust these niggas or bitches. You hear me," Kofi Jr. spoke with bass in his voice.

"I hear everything you are saying. Trust me," I assured them both.

The remainder of the ride Kevin Gates bumped through the system until we reached our destination. When the vehicle came to a complete stop, I spotted Judy's Vienna Red Hots located to the right of me. I got more excited about the food than my store.

"Let's go see your store, cuz. Then we got a few stops to make before we head back to the manor," Kaine mentioned. The three of us surveyed the area while we climbed out the Denali headed towards the store.

With each step closer to the building, I examined the exterior, including the fancy, white cursive writing in the window and the sign that read *Classic Curves Boutique*. Kaine handed the key to me so that I'd have the pleasure of entering first. Eagerly I entered the key into the lock, twisted it, and pushed the door open. The aqua wall color was easy and pretty on the eyes as I entered for a full walk-through. There were tiered display tables, shelves, dressed mannequins in a selection of summer items, and boxes on top of boxes with a selection of clothing items. The store also had two dressing rooms with a few body mirrors located on various walls.

"Pops had us to do a few things to get you started, but there are racks of clothes in the back. Bro and I need to go collect from these niggas, so we're gonna leave you here for an hour to arrange shit the way you want. Keep the blinds closed and the door locked until we get back," Kofi Jr. instructed.

"Aye, it's a strap inside the drawer behind the counter in case of emergency, only for an emergency," Kaine clarified.

"I got it! Now get out so that I can get some work done and convert this place."

"Alright, we love you. One hour," Kofi Jr said, putting up his index finger.

When they left, I locked the door and headed straight to the back room curious to view the clothes. Although I didn't pick out much of the merchandise, I'll admit the mixture of sundresses, shorts, tops, and swimsuits were popular name brand items. Each item was made for females of all sizes and shapes. Satisfied with everything in the back, I went back to the front to buss a move. To motivate myself, I got some music playing and before I knew it, the first three shelves filled with assorted graphic tees.

Still, in awe, my love for Uncle K and his willingness to keep me happy meant the world to me. His method of raising children might have differed from others, but I'm grateful for the job he did in raising me as his own. Although I missed having my father teach me how to drive, chaperone field trips, or have trips together, Uncle K had my back and filled those shoes. It was for that reason that I wanted to make him proud, prove myself, and learn a craft.

---

EACH DAY I went to the store and worked a few hours at a time until the place was ready to open for business. Of course, Uncle K had to check it out before he gave the final go-ahead, which was an even trade-off. While he did his walk around inspection, I kept my fingers crossed because he tended to be hard to please at times.

"Sooo, what do you think?" I asked not able to contain my anxiousness. He remained silent before turning in my direction.

"This is a big deal, so I'm trusting that you'll be a professional business owner."

"I promise not to let you down," I assured him and instantly wrapped my arms around his waist for a hug. Not big on showing affection, he gave me a quick squeeze and before easing me back.

"This is just the first phase. Your real challenge begins when you open those doors. Remember the goal is to make money. Finish up and get home, Estelle is cooking up a feast tonight," he added.

"I sure will. Her cooking is the bomb. Love you, uncle," I replied then gave him a peck on the cheek.

I watched him stroll out of the store as his driver held the vehicle door open until he was seated inside. Not too much longer after he'd driven off, Kaine stopped by to scoop me up. We made it home just as Estelle had placed the jerk chicken, yams, macaroni and cheese, and cornbread on the rectangle mahogany table. Estelle had been our personal chef for as long as I could remember, but she only cooked for us five days per week and on special occasions.

"Damn, I'm about to murder this food," Kaine mumbled as I had thought the same thing.

"Shit me too," Jr. chimed in, appearing out of thin air.

"I swear you smell food a mile away," Kaine teased Jr. while we waited for Uncle K to join us. Once he sat down, we joined hands, blessed the food, and filled our plates.

―――――――――

AFTER SURVIVING my first week of learning the ins and outs of the store world, I had officially become a store owner. Proud of the small accomplishment, I decided to go next door to order an Italian beef with the works and some fries. Judy's had the best ones, and they had some good ass burgers too. I waited for my order when this smooth brotha strolled inside. His skin tone was the same as mine, a honey golden yellow, which made him and his beard sexier. The smell of Ferragamo hit my nostrils prompting me to close my eyes to enjoy the scent.

"Excuse me, miss," he softly said on his way to the order window.

Right then the wheel in my brain began to spin as I tried to read the 6'8 hunk of gorgeousness that stood before me. He wore a navy blue Adidas jogging suit and was well-groomed and fresh looking.

"Let me get the ten-piece hot wings with fries and a side of okra. That will be all," he ordered then paid.

When that man turned around to reveal his full front side, my ass wanted to faint. Solid build yet not too buff; he was a snack that I wanted to add with my order.

"What you are smiling at over there?" he asked.

Caught off guard, I was unaware that I'd been smiling, so I played it off really quick. "I'm ready for this Italian beef, a sista's been craving one all week," I replied. We were the only two in the lobby, so he closed the space between us.

"I feel you. It's been a while since I've been to this joint since leaving the city. My ass will probably come back tomorrow to grab a big ass burger."

A few minutes went by as both of us retrieved our phones and stared at the screen. Indirectly I'd peep up to glance at him then quickly divert my eyes back down. Then my order was called at the pick-up window. Glad that my food was ready, I wasn't ready to cut the flirt fest short, so I couldn't help but glance one more time.

"Well take care, and I hope the food hit the spot. What was your name?" I questioned.

"I go by Lenox." He flashed those pearly whites making me clutch my pussy muscles. "What about you?"

"I'm Lani," I announced then bit my lip after revealing my real name, which was mistake number one.

"This might be too forward, but we should switch digits. You might want to recommend other food spots to a nigga."

We did just that, and thank goodness we did that shit quickly. The second we put our phones away the door swung open, it was my cousin. He strolled in like the cock block police ready to ruin my vibe. I just prayed he didn't embarrass me. Thinking fast I grabbed my food stuffing a few fries in my mouth so that I couldn't answer questions. Jr. instantly surveyed Lenox then diverted his attention my way, and opened the door as I marched out. On the way to the Denali, he finally spoke.

"You think you slick, cuz! You better make sure that nigga doesn't call you when any of us is around. Anyway, we need to head back to the mansion. I already doubled checked the store again," he affirmed.

"Dude, I swear y'all don't understand how jacked up it is that I gotta slip around with a male friend. If anything, y'all should glad I'm interested in men again," I voiced as he opened the door for me to hop inside.

While in the backseat, I went in on that damn polish sausage not paying attention to nothing else. I kept the mess to a minimal not leaving anything left but trash. Stuffed like a turkey, I enjoyed the remainder of the ride glad to finally get home and free my stomach from the pants. I couldn't help but wonder if I'd see ole boy again. Finally, a sista had some excitement to look forward to if he frequented the joint.

---

FOR TWO WEEKS STRAIGHT, my routine repeated until each clothing item had been folded and hung. I even received a shipment of skinny jeans, leggings, and a variety of denim. Well aware of my task ahead, I welcomed the challenge. In the final stages before opening the door, my nerves got the best of me. Scared to fail at anything, my uncle taught me to give a hundred percent in anything I did. Sometimes I wished my parents could see how far I've come tell me how proud they were of me, anything at all. In an effort not to dwell on the past, I tried to plan for my future.

The following week, the grand opening turned out better than I expected. Most of my customers were preteen and older teenage girls. The older girls purchased a majority of the sundresses. I watched while they shopped and giggled with one another. It was nice to see young girls enjoy their Saturday spending money in my store. By closing time I felt accomplished despite making less than three hundred dollars. When I made it home the first thing I did was search for Uncle K to give him a hug and kiss on the cheek. Afterwards, I grabbed a bite to eat, showered, rolled a blunt and turned on one of my all-time movies *Baby Boy*. Once I settled on the chaise I took a long drag of the blunt and held the smoke. I slowly exhaled the smoke and said aloud, "Today was a good day," in my Ice Cube voice.

---

FOLLOWING the daily debriefing with the family, I went ghost to soak in a lavender bubble bath for at least a half hour. The Jacuzzi tub relaxed my body as I indulged in the aroma of warm apple pie candles. After a few more minutes, my wrinkled fingers signaled it time to get out. I carefully climbed out of the tub, dried off, and applied Victoria's Secret Love Spell lotion all over my body. I slipped on the Victoria Secret pajama set with a pair of soft socks to match. Like clockwork, I retrieved water and then a joint from my stash box and lit it up. I inhaled the elicit smoke enjoying the sweet taste of the potent plant before exhaling. Cuddled up on the chaise with a fleece blanket, my phone went off, but I didn't rush to check it. Instead, the high from the OG Kush instantly relaxed my muscles and made me feel sedated.

*Buzz! Buzz!*

Vibration from the iPhone 7 Plus reminded me a message awaited my attention, so I picked it up off the ottoman. A message from Lenox's fine ass instantly made my nipples hard and panties wet like at Judy's. I used my right thumb to unlock it and read his text with a grin.

**Eye Candy:** *Hello, Miss Lady! I just ate a bomb ass Italian beef, and it made me think about you. What you up to tonight?*

**Me:** *Damn, that sounds good right about now too! I'm chilling back bored out my mind. About to watch this show called Ozark on Netflix about some dude who gets caught up when money laundering goes wrong.*

**Eye Candy:** *I never heard of it before, although I don't watch much of anything these days. I might have to check it out while I got a little downtime.*

**Me:** *So how long you plan to remain in town?*

**Eye Candy:** *Unfortunately, longer than I planned. Business is a bit more complicated than I assumed.*

**Me:** *Not to sound selfish, but I'm glad. Maybe we can chop it up in person sometime soon.*

I couldn't believe how long we texted each other back and forth or the fact I'd gotten myself into a tricky situation. Officially lit with a delayed reaction, I laid still as the background noise from the television sounded. Shortly a munchie attack kicked in resulting in me eating two Kit Kat candy bars followed by sixteen ounces of cold water. Almost a quarter to one in the morning, I tuned into a rerun episode of *Martin* when Jr. hit me up.

**Jr:** *You up? I noticed a light on from your window*

**Me:** *Hey. Yeah, I'm up.*

**Jr:** *I'm coming to visit if you're staying up for a minute. Don't send me off, cuz lol.*

**Me:** *Nigga, I'll be woke. Aye, you should bring me a bag of Flamin' Hots from the kitchen. Thank you in advance.*

**Jr:** *Yo ass high.*

**Me:** *LOL.*

I laughed aloud as I got up to stretch my legs and empty my bladder before Jr. made his way up. I washed up then returned to the chaise not able to stop thinking about Lenox and how to slip and see him. In debate within myself to ask Jr. for his help, it could only go in two directions. He'd help or not. In anticipation of his arrival, anxiety crept back on me not sure how to ask him to help me see a random nigga none of us knew.

*Knock! Knock! Knock!*

"It's open, dude!" I yelled out watching the door.

"What ya ass been up to?" Jr. asked upon entering. Ahh, OG Kush, yo ass is over there zotted.

"Hell yeah, bored too. I hate this damn insomnia shit, so I've been chilling. What you been on?" I asked, engaging in small talk.

"Business shit then Kaine and I went to tag team these sisters," he answered without a drop of embarrassment.

"Y'all ain't shit," I joked.

"Aye, you wanna blow?" he asked, pulling out two perfectly rolled blunts.

"Why not," I grabbed one not wasting time to light it.

In the midst of this, my phone vibrated again. This time the screen was face up. Jr.'s nosey ass snatched it before me. Messages were set to display on the screen then quickly disappear.

"Eye Candy?" he teased, looking at me. "This that yellow nigga, ain't it? Homeboy gonna get fucked up texting this late. These are booty call hours. You better let him know."

"First of all, give me my damn phone." I snatched it from his hand. "Second, why can't I have a friend? Y'all treat me like a damn five-year-old, but please remember I'm grown. You and K can tag team bitches, but I can't chat with a dude. Please," I hissed, relighting my blunt.

"Cuz, it doesn't matter how old or grown you get, we gonna treat you like a little sister. I'll admit it's foul that pops got you on a short leash," he admitted.

"Thank you. Aye, can we chat about something?" I inquired.

"What about?" Jr. questioned. "That nigga from Judy's? He certainly had his eye on you."

"Yeah, that brotha was fine," I joked knowing that it would piss Jr. off.

"Watch it," he warned.

"Unable to communicate or interact with folks other than family is lame. At least let me entertain myself. I'm trying to chill with dude just for a little bit, just talking obviously over food. You gonna help me?" I questioned with my famous stare down.

"Lani I'm not about to help a nigga get close to you. Nope," he refused. He tried to be hard but tended to give in sooner or later.

"All I want to do is eat a big ass burger in the company of a male companion, nothing more nothing less. Either way, my mind is made up, so ponder that, cousin." I knew he'd eventually help once I made the statement.

"You a little spoiled smartass chick, you know that? Dang, I'll help but believe if pops find out, I'll denying everything."

"Yes!" I exclaimed. When Jr. finally left, I hit Lenox back before the Sandman showed his ass and whisked me into a coma-like sleep.

# NINE

# LENOX SCOTT

Lani caught a nigga's eye, but the fool who came through the door had a serious problem. I didn't know who the fuck he was, nor did I care for his demeanor. It made me think twice about keeping her number in my phone. That type of drama wasn't what I needed since my pops had already roped me back into his street bullshit. Since my return to the city, there weren't many of my crewmembers left. Them niggas were either dead or in jail.

I needed ears on the street but couldn't trust a soul who wouldn't double cross me. Instead, my ass went old school and ear hustled to find out what I needed to know. Certain neighborhoods had gossiping ass young cats that couldn't hold water and were the type who ran their mouths. In need to find out who put the hit on my father, I kept my ears wide opened. Pops told me to pay Omar, also known as OG, a visit before I made any moves. I reached out and waited for a response.

OG and my pops went back to the hustling days cutting grass, plowing snow, raking leaves, and anything legit. Those legit jobs turned illegal and ultimately led to the drug business. Almost like another uncle, I went to him for advice whenever my pops became difficult, or if I needed reasonable sound advice. He kept all the street kids in line making sure we made kept spending money in our pocket. Come to think of it, OG even talked to me about sex, something my pops tried to do. His advice got me backhanded by this chick named Brittany, who is the reason that I approach females slightly different as an adult.

Thoughts of Brittany got me to thinking about that pretty young thang I met. You ever hold the phone in your hand contemplating on calling or texting someone? I sat on my bed not able to stop thinking about that chick from the food spot. Shorty was fine as fuck, so much so that it was worth a shot at reaching out to see what was good her way. To avoid looking thirsty, I searched for the right words to text, but that shit was harder than it should have been. It had been years since I'd thought about entertaining a woman, so I had no clue how to make the appropriate approach.

The munchies had kicked in, and my taste buds craved something from Judy's, so I made a quick dash to the spot, placing my order over the phone. By the time that order came through, that Italian beef didn't stand a chance. Before pulling out the lot, I took three bites then stuffed my mouth with a few fries. That food was so damn good, my craving ceased, but the face of ole girl popped in my head. In a hurry to get back to my pops crib, I drove fast enough, but at the speed limit.

**Me:** *Good evening, beautiful! Just wanted to drop a message to let you know you were on my mind. Hit me back. Lenox*

**Queen:** *Hey there! It's nice to be thought of by a stranger, j/k. Thanks for the message. I didn't think you'd be brave enough to message me after the way my cousin mugged the hell out of you. He does it all the time. Sorry.*

**Me:** *Ha, that explains the look. It's all good. I've encountered worse. So, what's the chance of seeing you again? I'd love to chop it up with ya over food or something.*

**Queen:** *Umm, that would be great, but my schedule is so tight* *that it's hard to say. Maybe you could swing by my shop one day soon or something.*

**Me:** *A young entrepreneur too? You got it going on, sweetheart! I love to see women about her business. What type of store?*

**Queen:** *It's a clothing store for girls and women, cute and affordable items that help keep a female's confidence.*

Against my better judgment, I took Lani up on her offer to visit her store even though it wasn't shit for me to buy. I parked across the street but lingered momentarily before finally climbing out the black Lexus ES. In motion towards Lani's spot, I entered as the ding from the bell above alarmed her of my presence.

"We meet again, beautiful! It's nice to lay eyes on you again. Relying on my memory was getting to be a challenge," I greeted Lani.

Her bright smile and pearly whites proved she had been happy to see me again too. In a deep glance over, she had been more attractive now than before. Next, to my mother, she had to be the finest woman I'd met. Those exotic eyes and plump lips were major a major turn on to me.

"Hi. It's really good to see you again too," she reciprocated the vibe. "Welcome to my clothing store. I have items for women of all sizes and shapes. Browse around; maybe you'll see something for the woman in your life."

"Although there is no woman, I'll still check out your merchandise." I slowly strolled through the cute establishment in an effort to please her. Truthfully, all I wanted to do was sit across from her and share a meal and conversation.

"Umm, I was thinking maybe we could grab something to eat from next door then go in the back to enjoy each other's company. What ya think?"

Lani's words were as if she read my mind or something so naturally, I agreed to her suggestion. "Aye, before we do, where is your cousin? I'm not down for the drama, ma," I made it clear to her.

"We good, I promise. My cousin is cool now, and he agreed to give me a little space. But trust, he's somewhere close per my uncle's instructions."

"Alright, let's go," I insisted as she led the way outside.

While we waited on our orders inside Judy's lobby, I probed to learn more about her. Within a short time, I learned she had a powerful uncle who made sure she remained with a male at all times. If I had to guess, her family was big time in drugs, real estate, or something. When we returned from next door with our food, she led me to the back of the store to what I presumed to be a break room. Inside, the left portion of the room had been filled with clothes and other store related stuff. To the right was a kitchenette type of setup where we took a seat. I examined the rest of the space to ensure that no one would jump out with an element surprise. That's when that funny feeling disappeared leaving me at ease.

"You have a cute and unique store here. It's something to be proud of, ma. I wish more of our young sistas would pursue their dream; you feel me? Stop working for these white men who see a slave or the Asians who pay under the table yet accuses you of stealing."

"Thank you. I agree. There are some talented females out here who got skills doing hair, nails, making clothing, and all that. It's not always easy though if the person is financially strapped."

She sure wasn't shy to eat in front of me. I loved a woman who acted the same around a man. Mesmerized by how she bit into her polish made my man rose a little in my pants as I imagined her lips around it. A nigga didn't want to think sexual but couldn't help it because she was irresistible. Determined to get in her panties, I just didn't know how to pull it off.

"Aye, this may be a weird question, but do you have a bathroom? I need to brush my teeth to kick this onion smell. I can't have bad breath ma," I confessed as I collected my trash and shoved it into the plastic bag.

"It's not weird just out the blue. I've never met a brotha who traveled with a toothbrush."

I removed the travel size toothbrush and tube of toothpaste from the inside pocket of my coat. She smiled and raised an eyebrow as she removed herself from the table to retrieve her bag. My eyebrows rose unsure why she got up until she raised her hands to display her pink travel size toothbrush and toothpaste. We shared a good laugh amazed at how similar we were.

"Wow. They say great minds think alike. People can't say we got bad breath," I commented. We chuckled again as she led me to the single stall restroom where we took turns freshening our breath.

"Let's do the breath test," I dared her in the spare of the moment. It had been the perfect moment to have her alone in a small space.

"Oh, you wanna see who got the freshest minty smell. Bring it on," she challenged.

I backed her up against the wall and slowly tilted my head and leaned in to kiss her. Without resistance, she reciprocated, engaged in lip play as she allowed my hands to roam across her breasts. Light moans crept from her mouth as she reached for my dick, which had come to full attention. She allowed me to unbutton her blouse in order to grip and suck her perfectly round titties better. Beyond aroused, I unbuttoned her pants and tugged them down to her ankles on a quest to her love box. Just as I placed my face near her pussy, the sweet smell of vanilla hit me.

"Wait!" she whispered and pushed my head back.

"What's wrong? I thought you wanted this, ma?"

"Shit, I do but—" I cut her off and stood up to stare her in the eyes.

"Damn ma, you see what you've done? My shit is so hard I gotta buss real bad." I took her hand and placed it on my hard rod. "Let me taste you so that I'll have something keep me going while I'm away," I tried hard to persuade her into giving in to me.

As I waited for her response, my hands rubbed that fat cat of hers, causing her to moan again.

"Ahh, that feels good! Damn, you got a smooth touch," her words trailed off as I slipped a finger inside her dripping wetness.

A few strokes later, my tongue replaced my finger, and I went to work on her shit. Lani's sweet juices damn near choked my ass, but luckily, my beard caught some of that shit. In the perfect position, I beat my meat and stroked Lani until I'd reached my peak and she screamed. I prayed she didn't have any STDs or diseases. Otherwise, it was over for a playa.

"Oh my goodness, please don't think I'm a hoe because of what we just did. It's been four long years since I've felt the pleasures of a man. My weakness got the best of me," she explained while pulling up her pants.

I stood up and immediately washed my face and brushed my teeth again. I watched her through the mirror. She was beauty in motion. Shit, I had to fuck her sooner than later.

"Look, ma. I'm not one to judge. No one is perfect. Besides, I'm glad that we did what we just did. I'll be honest. It's been a while for me too. It's hard to find a well-rounded woman who wants more in life besides material items."

"This is crazy. I've never done anything like this before in my life. I feel easy and cheap," Lani spoke with her back faced towards me.

"Aye we're grown, and we both wanted it. Shit, I know I did. Honestly, I wish it didn't have to end. That was an appetizer baby, and now I need to give you the full meal."

"Umm... In that case, we definitely need to hook up again."

"Aye, I better get up out of here before your cousin pops up ready to shoot me. Thank you for the meal and sample."

"You're all good. Be careful and hit me up later," she insisted.

I made it across the street not wasting time sliding in my ride pulling off. My left hand gripped the steering wheel flashes of Lani nearly caused me to run a red light. *Damn, nigga get yo' head together and pay attention to the road*, the little voice echoed. The horn blaring from a Honda Civic behind me prompted me to hit the gas pedal. The little beat up car suddenly dipped into the left lane as a white man flipped the bird not getting far. We got stuck again at another

red light. I let my window down then took my .9mm from my side
and raised it at him.

"What's the fucking problem punk?" I taunted.

His bitch ass quickly faced forward ready to speed the hell away.
That cracker zipped off so fast switching lanes in an attempt not to
catch a bullet. I hated disrespectful ass people.

---

FOCUSING on the reason that I made the trip into town, my pops
mentioned the Center Street Crew. Apparently, they are also
connected to the Burleigh Boyz and the Kingston Crew. All three
operated together and broke bread defending their territory. My pops
had overstepped his boundaries according to their rules. I'd also
learned more about the Kingston Crew who was known as the royal
family of the east side. All of the street drama gave me a headache
mainly because of who the key players were involved. In a difficult
situation to do right or wrong, I had plenty of shit to ponder before I
made moves.

In need of a more pleasant distraction, I decided to hit Lani sexy
ass up ready for another round of play. Although mysterious, she definitely had sex appeal, not to mention a juicy thang. Every time I went
into a bathroom thoughts about our rendezvous last week diverted to
her and how little I knew about her.

**Me:** *What's good, queen!*

**Queen:** *Hey there! This is a nice surprise text.*

**Me:** *As this song goes, "Someone's thinking of you, somewhere in
the world." You were on my mind. A brotha can't even go into the
bathroom without getting excited.*

**Queen:** *:-)*

**Me:** *Oh, you think it's cute, huh? Aye, if you're not busy let me
call so that I can hear that sweet voice.*

**Queen:** *Get to dialing. LOL.*

I read her message and let out a laugh then proceeded to dial her number. She had me doing something out of my norm, caking on the phone. That was female shit, but since we couldn't physically see each one another, it had to do.

"Say something sweet to me," I spoke into the phone when she answered.

"You got a great tongue," she said then giggled.

"And you taste deliciously pleasant."

"What you up to for the day?"

"I have to head back home for a week to catch up on a few things, but I'll be back soon. That's the price of owning a business. When I return maybe we can do something special."

"That would be great and long overdue. Where do you live anyway? It must be better than the Milwaukee," she assumed.

"I live in a small town named Blackwater. Before you ask, yes, black people live there too. The change in environment actually did me well."

"Where the hell is Blackwater located?"

# TEN

# LANI KINGSTON

Never did I plan to exchange anything but words with the man I'd barely known. Unable to think about anything but Lenox between my legs had my mind all over the place for the rest of the evening. When Lenox left the store, I reopened it only to gain four more customers before official closing at seven p.m. Distracted during the ride home Jr. played music as I glared out the window reliving my moment with Lenox.

"Aye Lani, you quiet over there. Talk to me," he insisted.

"Huh? Oh yeah, I'm okay, just tired that's all," I replied, lying through my teeth.

"Okay. Well, you wanted to keep busy, so your wish came true. We'll be home soon," he affirmed as he kept driving bobbing his head to Kevin Gates.

I had vowed never to fall for another man after Justin, but Lenox came into my life. Unexpectedly our encounter at Judy's and frequent texts and calls gave me something to look forward to at night. It was pure excitement. I was so attracted to him that spontaneous and magical moment made me want more.

The two of us grew closer and closer, and he had damn near

spent a thousand dollars in my store. He admitted that all of the clothes he purchased were donated to a group home for girls. His charming giving demeanor was a major turn on, not to mention the physical, sexual attraction. I'd never wanted to fuck so badly, but under my circumstances, the opportunity never presented itself. Justin had been my one and only, so imagine not experiencing the pleasures he'd once introduced me to.

It had come to the point that my body wanted, no my body needed that same attention from Lenox. It had become impossible to be around him and not drool or orgasm. In a way, our secret hook-up turned me blind and made me head over heels. I'd begin to forget everything my cousins and uncle taught me about men. Our arrangement to meet at the store went on longer than expected. I never mentioned to anyone that he lived in Blackwater, which is the same place Aunt Ruthie lived. I wondered if they were related or if it had been coincident. My thoughts spiraled, not sure what to think when he first shared that piece of information.

Once my uncle found out, he forbid me to see Lenox again. Of course, Jr. denied any knowledge just as he promised. Pissed for three days at my uncle's controlling ways, I hid out in my suite where I rolled up and sparked blunts. Smoking always eased my mind and body. Not long after I got into chill mode, Lenox hit my line. I felt my cheeks spread from the schoolgirl blush he gave me.

"What it do, boo!" I answered lounging on the chaise.

"Ma, you are funny. I just wanted to hit you up before turning my phone off. I have to take care of some shit but needed to hear that sweet voice."

"That's thoughtful. I'm chilling, bored as shit. My uncle is driving me nuts holding me hostage," I complained.

"What you mean? You can't just leave when you want to leave?"

"No. It's complicated. He has forbidden me from seeing you again. He found out about our meal dates at the store."

"I'm sure he only has your best interest and safety at heart. Don't be hard-headed, keep ya butt inside," he demanded.

"I guess the men have spoken," I remarked sarcastically. "It's not like I have a choice, huh."

"Alright queen, I'll hit you back tomorrow. Stay sweet!"

"Aww, you are so sweet! Be safe. Chat tomorrow," I said back to him wishing the call didn't have to end.

I tossed my phone aside on the bed and let the effects of the Indica plant put my body in a sedation state. Mentally I schemed on a new way to slip and see Lenox regardless of what my uncle forbid me to do. Disobeying my uncle never got easy, but when it came to something I wanted, it fueled my desire to get it.

---

TIME SPENT at the store proved to be more work than I anticipated, but never did I admit it to my uncle. He'd been a firm believer in seeing a project, job, or task all the way to the end. In my case, his expectations were higher because it was my idea and he backed me financially.

I'd gotten into a groove each day when getting ready for the work-day. It reminded me of the hospital days. The business started slower than I hoped, but a few customers a day was better than none at all. Aware that a small business was a financial risk, my goal to make money would prove to the family of my skills. It was Friday, so I prayed a few folks would spend some of their work check on merchandise in my store.

Not able to fold another item, I took a break and pulled out my iPad for a few games of Bingo Bash. The sound of the bell alerted me someone had entered. My head shot up as I greeted the customer. "Welcome to Classic Curves Boutique. Browse around and let me know if you need any assistance."

"Good afternoon. It's some cute stuff in here," the female voice commented.

I slid the iPad to the side and stood up from the stool to assist the woman who had begun to browse. The closer I got to the butterscotch woman, the more she resembled someone I used to know.

"KK?" I called out not sure if it was her. I hoped she didn't think I was nuts calling her a random name. The woman looked up at me squinted her eyes before she realized we knew each other.

"Lani?" the familiar voice spoke up.

"Yes. It's me, KK. It's been so long yet you still look the same. It is great to see an old friend." We embraced each other with a quick hug.

"Girl, you are looking good these days. You've even filled out," she joked.

"Four years make a difference. So how you been?" I questioned. "Are you still at the hospital?"

"Hell naw girl. I had to give that place the deuces. Now I'm at the funeral home on Hampton Avenue."

"Northwest Funeral Chapel," we both announced in unison.

Those words brought a sick feeling to my stomach as my mouth watered in the process. It dawned on me that was the exact place where Justin's service was located. Not sure if KK's pop up and the mentioning of her new job was pure coincidence or not, I tried to shake off the unpleasant feeling.

"Umm... Did I say something wrong? You look ill," KK questioned.

"I'm fine. It's just the same place where my fiancé Justin..." my words trailed off as I got choked up.

"Oh no, I'm sorry Lani I didn't realize, please forgive me," KK quickly apologized.

"It's okay. Browse around while I step in the back for a sec," I insisted and rushed to the back.

In need of a moment, I entered the bathroom, stood over the sink, and splashed my face twice with cold water. In a better state of mind, I returned to find KK with an arm of selected tops and graphic tees.

"Hey, girl." I walked over to her with a smile plastered on my face.

"Honey, I found some cute stuff for my niece. I better get the hell out of here before I spend too much," KK joked and made her way towards the cash register.

"I know that's right," I agreed while I rung up each item and placed them in the turquoise gift bag. After the payment transaction, I stepped from behind the register to exchange one last hug.

"Lani it was great seeing you girl. Hey, what's your number? We need to have lunch or something to catch up." She slid her phone from her pocket and handed it to me to enter my digits. I pressed the green phone icon to call my phone then hung up and saved my name in her contact list.

"I'm all in for that, honey. All I do is work and stay home bored," I agreed quickly.

"I'd love to reconnect like we used to do. Spending time with dead bodies is nice and all but chile I need some interaction," she remarked. Immediately she covered her mouth after realizing her continuous mentioning of death.

"It's okay. I'm better now. Have a good evening, and I look forward to hooking up soon."

Jr. strolled into the store just as she was about to exit, and I was glad it happened. Within that short moment, I'd realized KK could help me with the plan I'd devised to see Lenox.

"Aye, that's shorty from St. Joseph's right? Dat ass got big since the last time."

"Jr., stop playing. Yeah, that's her, nice surprise right? Now I got another female to talk and text."

"You ready to roll out?"

"Yup, give me ten."

I performed my tasks then locked up before climbing into Jr's truck.

In the passenger side, I contemplated how to persuade my uncle into letting me drive myself around. My Benz had been sitting in the garage collecting dust for over six months. Apparently, in the middle of brainstorming, I'd drifted off during the ride, which usually took half an hour. When the motion stopped my eyes automatically popped open, a sign, we had made it to our destination.

"Wake yo big headed ass up. We home," Jr. announced.

"No shit Sherlock," I shot back at him still blinking as my pupils adjusted to the bright lights. Instead of confronting my uncle, I decided against it until the next morning when we were both fresh.

"Night, love you."

---

THE NEXT MORNING I woke up minutes before sunrise feeling refreshed. I went to the bathroom and handled my hygiene, dressed, and made the trip to the kitchen. Not too hungry I grabbed an apple from the bowl that sat on the kitchen island. Quietness filled the room until the sound of the back door closed.

"Morning, beautiful niece," Uncle K mumbled through heavy breathing. He had just come back from a run on the tracks.

"Morning dear uncle, I see you up early getting it in. That's good. Maybe I should start joining you twice a week," I joked.

"That would be nice. I'll take you up on that challenge."

While he turned his back towards me to grab a water bottle, I decided to use the opportunity to ask about my driving. When he turned to face me, I had the biggest Kool-Aid smile on my face.

"Oh shit, what you want now girl?" he questioned, giving me that look.

"Just a thought, it's time to get my Benz serviced so that I can drive myself around. You spent a grip on that truck only for it to sit and collect dust. Besides, my driver's license doesn't expire until 2022."

"I swear you will convince a man to slit his own wrist. You a force young lady. I see a bright future. I'll have Sean take care of it first thing. Anything else while I'm in a generous kind of mood?" he asked.

"Nothing at all, dear uncle. Thank you for always coming

through despite my hardheadedness. Love you." I placed a kiss on his cheek, leaving a lip ring.

"Love you too, honey. Now go away. I got business to tend." He left the kitchen in one direction, and I headed in another excited about driving again.

# ELEVEN
# KINGSTON JR

My life revolved around the family business, my siblings, and getting paid 24/7. Although each day was a risk for me when I left outside those gates, I no doubt loved what I did. A hustler by default I was also an educated muthafucker with a degree in Video Game Development and Programming. Developing games turned out to be my side interest as a teen until I convinced my father to let me pursue the hobby. Before I got in deep with the family business, my hobby turned into paid tournaments across the Midwest. An experience of a lifetime, I played with some of the best gamers online.

I played "First of the Month" by Bone Thugs- N- Harmony while I made his rounds to collect money from the different pick-up spots. That joint could never get old to me. The first stop was at the check cashing and corner store spot on Center Street. I hopped out the whip and ran inside to pick up the case of Pringles chip containers from the owner. I checked each stash can to ensure all money was inside then proceeded to several spots and did the same thing. Those Pringles stash cans were used as a cover to make sure police had no reason to fuck with me. By the time I finished collecting, my back seat was filled with a variety of chip cans.

Just as I hopped in the truck, my phone started blowing up the screen displayed a name that didn't interest me. I ignored the call and drove off headed to count the money. Desirae was nothing but a headache to a nigga. I met her over a year ago on some thot drunk shit one night. Shorty ass caught my eye first because she was so fucking stacked. She had a Serena Williams ass that made a grown man cry. The sista had a smooth, milk chocolate complexion, bad body, and personality. After two fucks, I learned why the hell niggas hit and split. Shorty turned out to be clingy as hell. That type of shit didn't fare well with me. A nigga like me needed freedom.

Later that night once business had been conducted Kaine talked me into being his sidekick while he tried to impress some chick. He knew blind dates always turned out to be a bad idea, but because he asked, my answer was yes. For the first time in a long time, that Kingston urge didn't provoke me to fuck any random chicks. Typically, a few drinks and a little coke left me doing wild shit, but something hit me. The blind date turned out to be an attractive chick, but she didn't turn me on not one bit. However, her facial features and side profile favored that of a chick that I'd been exclusively dating. Kaine, on the other hand, got what he wanted by the end of the night, and I sure as hell didn't hate.

---

KAINE AND KD held shit down on the business side while I decided to slide over my main chick's crib for some quality time. She understood business always came first no matter what happened. Opposite of Desirae, Diva never blew my phone up or talked recklessly as a way to keep me around. Instead, she was my peace, a person I enjoyed to be around when the street shit got hectic. Although Diva had semi earned my trust and gave a nigga keys to her crib, I never shared personal shit in case she was working for our archenemy.

Diva lived on 76th and Good Hope in an area where people

stayed to themselves. Before parking, I tended to circle her block twice to make sure nobody had been following me or waiting to catch me slipping. When I knew the coast was clear, I exited my truck and let myself inside her single family home.

"Damn, I'm glad to see yo' black ass," was the first thing out of Diva's mouth as she approached the door.

"Chill yo' ass girl, I'm here now!" I spat as I locked the door behind me.

"I cooked just in case you hungry. Otherwise, bring that ass to me now," she demanded.

I strolled up to her placing kisses on those luscious lips that were plump and glossy causing me to get hard. Whenever she glossed them, I could imagine my dick between them. The most beautiful feature on a woman, Diva's lips enticed the fuck out of me. I could feel her hand reaching for my manhood.

"You want this dick, huh? Let the dick slayer give you all the dick you want. You about to feel this shit in yo stomach, girl!"

"Hell yeah, I do. Stop playing and serve me up, baby. It's been way too long since you beat this shit," she said lustfully.

"Since you put it that way let's do it. You lead, and I'll follow behind you." I smacked her on the butt as we went the short distance to her bedroom. It had been almost two weeks since we had a chance to hook up, so I needed assistance.

"Be naked by the time I come out. I'm about to tear that ass up! You might wanna do a few stretches while you at it."

"Oh shit, you finna put in some work. Hurry ya ass up," she shot back, stripping out of her clothing.

I closed the bathroom door and removed the small orange plastic tube from my pocket in need of a bump. I flipped the top, poured a white line on the back of my hand, and snorted it. Nobody knew of my once in a while habit, not even Lani who spent more time with me than anybody else. Cocaine made the sex greater, electric and increased my sensory, but most of all my drive increased. Diva required all my energy. She tended to be a firecracker that was hard to contain at times.

When I opened the door, Diva greeted me with titties swinging and a freshly shaved pussy. I sniffed in anticipation of what was about to take place for the next two hours. Satisfied with the visual and no longer able to wait I scooped her up diving my face into her breasts, taking one in my mouth. She always craved that type of thing. It always got her hot and bothered. Next, she unfastened my belt, not wasting time freeing my dick from my boxers.

She dropped to her knees and took my meat in her hands gently toying with it before she shoved it into her warm moist mouth.

"Ahh!" I groaned. Her tongue did circles around the tip a few times before she started to get down. Wet and sloppy just the way I liked it, I held my head back as she worked her jaws overtime.

"Can't nobody do this shit better than you girl! DAMN!" I shouted trying hard as fuck not to explode yet. I swear her mouth was like a microwave, convenient and quick to get the job done. The sounds of her slurping me down filled the room just as she sucked the sperm from shit. "Ooh, shit you got a dangerous weapon!" I said through moans.

"That was faster than usual. I guess you were excited to see me. Let me go wash my mouth right fast. I'm ready to feel you deep inside me," she confessed, springing to her feet as she disappeared momentarily.

When Diva returned, she seductively moved towards me as if I was her prey, precisely making calculated strides until our bodies became one. I wrapped my arms around her waist placing kisses on her stomach. A faint smell of her Prada perfume still lingered, and the fragrance drove me crazy. I rubbed between them juicy legs, a clear sign she was ready to ride.

"You should take them fucking shoes off so that we can really have some fun," Diva hissed.

"Come on now. You already know a nigga don't come out the

kicks, anything can pop off. You promised not to bring this up again, don't ruin the mood, baby," I added.

"I know, it's just weird fucking somebody who's not bare ass like me. Forget I even mentioned it," she sucked in her teeth.

"Girl stop pouting and come jump on this dick," I ordered.

It was apparent she felt some type of way, but it didn't matter to me because she still couldn't resist me. In anticipation, Diva straddled me.

Before I entered her, a nigga double-checked the condom making sure it was on then she gradually devoured my dick making it vanish inside of her. Two thrusts inside her made me see stars as the soft velvet feeling of the pussy gripped my shaft. Excited, a nigga didn't want to explode right away. Those chocolate nipples of hers were perfect for sucking on too.

Whenever she rode me I damn near lost my mind, she had a habit of contracting them pussy muscles, gripping my rod. I felt every single twitch with each grind and thrust. Baby used to be a dancer, talk about suburb balance and leg strength.

"Shiiit, you know how to pop this pussy!" I called out unable to keep my outbursts to myself.

"You truly are the dick pleaser baby. This dick feels amazing, but I need you to hit me doggy style now. Can you handle that boo?"

"You ain't said nothing but a word Ms. Thickums, bring that ass," I commented while we changed positions.

There was no better way to fuck a bitch with a big ass doggy style. She bent over as I slid inside the warmth like it was home, gradually going in and out at a decent pace until the urge came down. It was something about them cheeks slapping against me as I pounded harder and harder.

"YES!" Diva exclaimed.

That motivated me to put in work going into autopilot. I slapped her ass, pulled her hair, and did anything else I could as the orgasm almost sent my body overboard into a sexual peak.

Before long, my stroke went deep, exploring her walls. It was nothing like hot, wet, gushy stuff. "When you squeeze and release them pussy muscles gah, oh shit I get weak."

"Don't cum yet; this dick feels too good right now." Her dirty talk made me hard all over again. The motion of her body made it difficult to hold on.

"SHIT!" we both shouted, a clear sign we got each other off.

I pulled out making sure to hold the condom in place moving straight into the bathroom. Quickly I discarded the condom carefully, washed my joint off, and pulled my shit up. While fastening my belt, I returned to find Diva headed in my direction.

"Move nigga, I gotta pee," she hissed followed by laughter.

"Oh what you hit me with the *White Chicks* scene," I joked.

I checked my phone to find a text from KD. Just as I was about to read it, I felt a pair of hands. I locked my screen and turned around to face her.

"Don't stay away long, boo! I need to be dosed up more often so think about that for next time," Diva's voice projected from behind me.

"It's never my intentions, but you know how it is, family and business always come before pleasure, but I hear you and will try to do better. I gotta get the hell out of here and head back home."

"I need to shower and take my ass to sleep anyway. I have a long work day ahead in the morning." She sighed.

"Shit, my workday never ends. I'll hit ya back sooner than later. Until next time, take care of yourself, ma," I expressed then placed a soft kiss on her forehead before exiting.

On the way down the steps, I looked to my left, then to my right, aware of my surroundings. Once I closed the car door the phone made an alert sound to remind me of the unread message.

*Beep! Beep!*

**KD:** *Bro, time to go put in that work. Two lame ducks need a visit.*

While I drove in search for Ty, my dirty mind imagined ways to have intimate moments with Diva. Thoughts of her seductive lips and eyes made a little pre-cum seep from my dick. It was a personal goal of mine to wife her ass up one day if I made it out the game. She cooked, sucked, and fucked on a superior level, better than any woman I'd ever met.

Dark by five o'clock, I finally found a location for that fool who had ping-ponged across Milwaukee. When I rolled up on him, it was no time to hear explanations, with my bitch in hand he ran into an alley.

"Nigga, did you really think there was a place in the hood you could hide? Kingston men hunt and find no matter what. Any last words bitch nigga?"

"It wasn't even me, dawg. That nigga Meech took the dope."

I stood over Ty with my chrome nine and let off three rounds in his head. "Meech's ass is next to don't worry," I stepped over his body and walked to my car.

Behind the wheel, I hit bro up to let him know half of the task was complete. Meech was harder to find because he paid everyone to lie. Damn near two hours later Kaden sent his location, and it was where I least expected. That nigga was hiding at the nursing home where his great auntie resided. Careful in my actions when I approached him, my respect for the old folks saved him from embarrassment for ten minutes. After that, he took a ride with me to his final resting spot, and I made it home to eat with my family.

# TWELVE
# LENOX SCOTT

Back in my hometown, I decided to check into the Iron Horse Hotel instead of going back to my pops spot. I needed extra space and privacy in case Lani, and I decided to get nasty. After getting settled, I took a leak, showered and gave my pops a quick call. Tired as fuck, my old ass got into bed, propped a pillow behind my head and tuned into ESPN. Although my body grew tired, my mind remained active. I hit Lani up for a chat session. Chicks gushed over shit like that, but I honestly enjoyed it too. In a short time, our connection grew to a point she had a nigga smiling and shit. I typed and sent the message off.

**Me:** *Guess who's back, beautiful! I can't wait to see you and that banging body again.*

**Queen:** *That's the best news I've gotten today! How long are you staying this time?*

**Me:** *A few weeks, maybe another month. Don't worry, we hooking up as soon as I'm free.*

**Queen:** *Looking forward to it. We gotta figure out a new plan to see each other since my uncle is on my ass about seeing you again.*

**Me:** *Well, I'm at the Iron Horse Hotel. It's my temporary home. I* *think they have a spa. Google that shit, and I know you'll come up with the perfect plan.*

**Queen:** *I sure will...*

**Me:** *Alright, hit me tomorrow. I need some shuteye. You do too, businesswoman! Good night.*

**Queen:** *Good night!*

---

OG FINALLY HIT ME BACK, so I decided to slide through to his spot for a quick visit. Before I could even park and turn the car off, he snatched the door open and stood shirtless with a Newport dangling from his lips. The closer I got the more visible his war scars and tattoos were visible on the forearms and the upper portion of his chest.

"Bring ya yellow ass on and give me some love."

Instantly I laughed because niggas had been giving me shit about being yellow since middle school. Up the stairs, I acknowledged him followed by a handshake. "How did you know I was here?"

"I got cameras all around this bitch and see it all. You know the rule, never get caught slipping," he noted.

"Shh, I hear you on that," I agreed.

"Aye man, it's good to see you again. Life must be treating you right."

"Thanks, OG! I try to live right that's all."

We entered his home as he led me down to the lower level where he chilled out to watch sports drinking beer. His basement was carpeted and cozy, almost set up like another apartment. He took a seat then gestured towards multiple gray loveseat recliners for me to do the same.

"OG these recliners are smooth. I might have to order one for my spot."

"Big enough to have ya main squeeze chill alongside you."

"So what the hell you been up to nowadays?"

"Ain't nothing changed my way, collecting cash and staying away from these dumbass millennials. Aye, I spoke to ya pops, and he filled me in on shit. How can I help?" he asked as I watched him light up a blunt."

"Yeah, he got me in his shit. I need to know more about these street crews before I react. The more, the merrier you feel me?"

"These streets are not like they used to be a youngin'. It used to be a certain level of respect. Some shit niggas just didn't do because of the street code. The whole crew got put on and ate well but now." He paused to inhale the strong trees, then exhaled and passed it my way. Before accepting, I contemplated if I should smoke, didn't want to get stuck for hours.

"Before I hit this, will a nigga be able to function within an hour? I gotta be mobile."

"You'll be straight. As I was saying, the game ain't changed but the players sure the hell did. These dummies need to be in school or engaged in some kind of trade."

"I feel you on that shit. Pops said the same thing in different words. So I need to know which crew got the most back up. Some of these cats won't step on a grape if they leader gets clipped."

"Cuz nobody knows who the main connects are personally, but it's all linked back to the Kingston Clan. That family is like the hood version of the Kennedys with all those damn boys. All of the street crews kicked a percentage of the profits back to Kingston Sr. in exchange for their life."

"They got it like that, huh?" I had a little buzz going intrigued in the conversation.

"It's about seven of them including a female, she either the sister or cousin. Back in the day, Kingston Sr. and I did business a few times. The shit was always clean and without incident. He's a businessman and killer, and he raised his offspring the same way."

"Wait, you said a female? What do you know about her?" I asked for the simple fact Lani always complained about her strict uncle.

"Umm, don't know much honestly. Shit nobody even knows

where they reside on the east side. What I can tell you is that they have blood ties to Jamaica, which means they're bat shit nuts."

"I think the female I've been fucking with is the same chick you mentioned. That shit all makes sense now. Whenever we chop it up, she complains that her uncle doesn't allow her to leave home alone. Then there's the time we met in Judy's, and her cousin threw me a hell of a mean mug."

Mind blown, all of our interactions replayed in my head, her texts and comments swirled as if a *Wheel of Fortune* puzzle had been solved. OG made me realize how little I knew about the woman who had begun to steal my heart.

"Damn, my nigga. It sounds like you closer to the enemy than you thought. Aye, you might as well get in deeper. Now you said you fucking with her, did you hit yet?"

"OG, you a fool man," I expressed. "Not yet. That might be my way to get further inside the family. Her uncle found out about our meetups, so of course, he doesn't want her seeing me."

"Well, whatever you do plan that shit down to the littlest detail. I got some soldiers who will suit up if needed. Let me warn you, cuz. Shit will get real nasty in the streets so if you really want to proceed. Sleep on that shit," OG demanded.

"You already know, I ain't scared, but I'm trying to avoid as much bloodshed as possible. Honestly, I'm more afraid of turning into the man I've tried hard for years not to be anymore. Well, like you said, I got a lot of thinking to do. Let me get my ass up out here and get to pops crib." Comfortable as hell, I slid out of the recliner and stood to my feet. OG did the same.

"It was nice to see yo ass and catch up. Don't forget what I told you now. Hit me when you decide on your plan," he noted while in motion to head back up the stairs to the main level.

Escorted back outside it had turned cloudy and chilly. I made me do a quick dash to the car. Quickly I started the ignition and cranked the heat and music then drove down the residential street.

Surprised Lani was the niece of drug supplier Kingston hurt me, only because I'd started digging the hell out of her before even having sex. She had never flat out told me who her uncle was nor did she reveal her last name. With the new information being a game changer, my approach to everything had to be precise.

Cruising down Center Street on the way to check in on pops, memories of playing basketball, and slanging and banging resurfaced. The young me was reckless and didn't give a fuck about anything. Life as a son of a big-time dealer tended to be fast speed, all I knew was hustling. The older me grew thankful as shit to still be alive, and I found a different type of hustle without a gun. I whipped into the driveway not wasting time getting inside the house. An idea popped into my head.

"Pops, I might have a solution, but it could turn into a problem if my plan doesn't work. The shit that I learned from OG has shed light on a personal conflict."

"What type of conflict?"

"I think the chick I've been slipping around with is the niece of Kingston Sr. Obviously he knows of me but not my identity. Anyway, if this is true, maybe I can use her to get close to him."

"What? You out here sleeping the enemy, son?" he asked in a confused tone.

"First off we haven't slept together yet, and as I said, I just learned this information. Hear me out," I encouraged him before he began to chew my head off. "If I can get close to her uncle and talk like grown businessmen, I'm hoping to handle shit in a nonviolent way."

"Nigga, you're not the modern day Martin Luther King Jr. These fools don't know the meaning of nonviolence. They kill for a living!" he spat, not feeling my approach.

"Damn, it's like that," I laughed because his comment caught me by surprise.

"Let's be for real. You know I'm telling the truth. What did OG suggest?"

"He told me to think hard before moving forward and if I need his soldiers ready whenever."

"That is music to my ears. I got a bad feeling shit about to hit the fan. I made a quick run to Walmart and could've sworn somebody was tailing me.

"Woah, tell me what happened and don't leave out any detail," I insisted.

"I made a quick run to the store to grab some fruit, laundry detergent, and other house items. Shit was smooth when I drove out the lot and drove through two sets of lights. By then I noticed a dark two-door car on my ass. Not sure if my paranoia had kicked in, I decided to deviate from my normal route home. Sure enough that ugly little car stayed behind, so naturally, I dipped down a few side streets until the car disappeared."

"Pops yo ass in too deep and can't keep living with a target on the dome. If somebody is tailing you, they want you bad. Is this just about you being ax man or did you do something else?"

"I already told you why don't keep questioning me. Whatever the situation, you supposed to have my back no matter what," he raised his voice almost in irritation.

"Yeah alright," I responded.

To avoid saying some shit that I shouldn't to him, my first mind told me to get up and leave.

"I'm out of here, have a good night," I expressed before closing the door behind me.

Being upset with my father made me realize why I left in the first place. We agreed to disagree, and it drove me wild. I headed back to the hotel for some isolation, meditation, and rejuvenation. In spite of my father's lack of faith, it made me even more determined to work shit out. In further thought, I had to make a promise to myself not to get involved with the drug life ever again if I walked away.

# THIRTEEN

# LANI KINGSTON

It had been a breath of fresh air to have KK back in my circle because the guys had almost driven me bat crazy. We chatted a few times after she came into the store in, which I filled her in on a few things worth sharing. As far as she knew, I'd owned the store and didn't do many outside appearances. I downplayed the part about my strict uncle who preferred my volunteer house arrest. By the time we finished, she had agreed to hop on board in helping make sure all loose ends were tied. KK seemed as if she did something similar once upon a time in her teen days. When we hung up, lunch and a spa day had been our official cover story. I sent Lenox the details my new partner in crime helped cook up.

In need to release all of the excitement inside, I decided to throw on my black Nike one-piece swimsuit. It had been at least a month since I had any interest to get in the water. I slipped into a pair of thong flip-flops and slipped on a pink terry cloth robe. With the pool located at the far left end of the hallway, the walk served as a mini leg workout. The smell of chlorine hit my nose the moment I set foot inside the enclosed space. Having motion controlled lighting, each panel turned on as I walked the non-slip floor.

"Hey Alexa, play swim playlist!" I yelled out, removed the robe and slipped out of my flip-flops. I stepped into the shower to wet my body, before diving into the crystal blue body of water.

To warm up, I swam two laps and took a rest, but when my nigga Kevin Gates came on, I did one lap easy and one lap fast repeating the same thing several times. After I felt like a mermaid the way, I glided back and forth from one end to the other. The water had gotten warm to the point that I didn't want to get out. When the playlist ended is when I slowly exited the pool lightly breathing. The room temperature had automatically adjusted to warm up space while I dried off and wrapped in my robe.

**Jr:** *Aye rock head your Benz is back from the dealership.*

**Me:** *YES! I can't wait to drive my baby tomorrow. It seems like forever since I drove myself.*

**Jr:** *Yeah, I'm glad to be off of driving Ms. Daisy duty. Pops must have been in a good ass mood to agree to this shit. Either way, you are winning!*

**Me:** *Shut up, nigga. Yeah, he was in a great mood. I got a lunch and spa date with KK. I'm turning in early. Luv you, cuz!*

**Jr.** *Damn, it's only 9:30 p.m.*

**Me:** *So. I got a business to run in the morning chump. LOL. Night, rock head.*

I tossed the phone on the bed and moved towards the nine-drawer dresser that had lights around the panel. While doing so, my reflection in the mirror prompted me to admire how much I favored my mother. She too had fair, flawless skin as a result of her creole DNA, which passed on to me. Oh how I missed her and my dad, frequently wondering what they would've thought about the life Uncle K provided for me. I let out a deep sigh, removed a nightgown, and shuffled my feet to the bathroom for a quick shower. After, I rubbed a light coat of cocoa butter over every inch of my body and slipped on the gown. By the time I hit the blunt and then the bed, it was already close to midnight.

THE NEXT MORNING I woke up sore as a bitch not realizing a month off had been a bad idea. My arms were the worse, but it didn't stop me from claiming a good day. Slowly but surely I climbed out the bed excited for the day ahead, almost like a kid on field trip day. The store business increased bit by bit, and the morning kept me moving the entire four hours. Just before my departure from the store, I hit KK up to inform her of my location.

BUTTERFLIES FILLED my stomach at the mere thought of seeing Lenox again since he licked me down. It's bad enough that my anxiety hit me while I drove, but it faded soon afterwards when the voice from the GPS announced that I had reached my location. The tall, brick hotel had a unique and historical style. It was the type of spot one could hide out unnoticed. I pulled into the valet, leaving the key inside for the female attendant who approached. Before climbing out, I did one last check in the rearview mirror to check my lipstick and teeth.

"Damn you, fine girl," I complimented myself as I slipped on my black Gucci oversized frames and stepped out.

"Good afternoon, ma'am," the valet politely greeted.

"Hi!" I greeted while strutting away with confidence over to a different servant for a ticket.

Not wanting to appear too sexy, I wore a black fitted Gucci pea coat with a gold double G belt and a knee-length striped dress to match underneath. Once inside the hotel, I removed my glasses to scan the lobby, then over to the bar and grill restaurant adjacent from the entrance. In Kingston fashion, I sashayed through the place as if I owned it until I finally found my girl sipping a long island.

"Hey chica, I finally made it," I greeted as she stood for a quick embrace. She stepped back to glance me over.

"Honey, you cute cute today, Gucci everythang," she sang then busted out in laughter.

"Girl thanks. You know I'm a designer freak." I removed my coat and took a seat ready to order a cocktail.

"Lani, girl, this place is huge. Until today, I didn't even know it was here. The menu items not too bad either. I told the waiter to give me fifteen, so he should be circling our way soon. Aye, excuse me but is that yo handsome ass cousin?"

Sure enough, it was Jr. moseying his ass towards us wearing a big ass grin on his face. I rolled my eyes in the air hoping that he didn't plan on hanging around long. In the search for the waiter, I really needed a drink.

"What you doing here? Spying on me," I questioned.

"I'm checking in on you. Hello KK, it's always nice to see you again." He kissed her hand, flirting just like the hoe he proved to be with the women.

"Umm, let go of her hand and stop trying to mack. Aye, for real though, here take a picture of us. I'm about to send this to Uncle K." He snatched the phone and took a few quick shots then hurried up and took a selfie with KK.

"Give me my damn phone," I said through gritted teeth then busted out laughing. While he tried to mack I sent the pictures to my uncle then sent the other one to Jr. "Alright it's time to leave us to our girl time, cousin darling," I fussed until he finally left.

The second Jr. departed, the waiter appeared to refresh KK's drink, get me a vodka and cranberry, and took our orders. While we waited, KK filled me in more on why she left the hospital and switched to working with dead people. It always interested me why some folks chose such professions.

"It's gotta be creepy sometimes being in a room with dead bodies. Have you had any strange encounters yet?" I questioned.

"I won't lie. It took me two weeks to get in a comfortable space, but now it's nothing to it. I play music, talk to them, and do my daily tasks. The toughest thing is seeing the condition some folks are in when they are put on the slab. Girl, you are too interested in this mess. Let's change topics to men."

"Girl, I'm kind of nervous but excited because it's been a minute since we've had alone time without my cousin hovering. We haven't had sex yet either so this whole situation got me feeling like a high school girl," I confided in her.

"Oh yeah you gonna need another drink, you'll be loose as a goose," KK joked as she sipped her drink.

"Here we go ladies," the man placed our plates in front of us.

In pure enjoyment of my company with KK made me realize how much of life I hadn't been living. Listening to her talk about the different jobs she had, boyfriends, and the freedom reminded me how young I was with so much to accomplish. The underlying issue reverted to the captivity of the mansion, which prevented me from exploring like KK. In mid laughter, my phone vibrated on the table causing me to check it.

**Eye Candy:** *I've been watching you from across the lobby. You have such a beautiful smile! The waiter will return to your table with a key to my room.*

**Me:** *Wow! How long have you been watching me?*

**Eye Candy:** *Long enough to watch you and your girlfriend erupt in laughter. I think it's cute you two are having fun. I'm we're about to have fun too upstairs. Enjoy your company. Hope to see you soon.*

**Me:** *Definitely! See you in a few!*

I placed my phone face down on the table to continue the last few minutes with my girl. For the first time in a very long time, I'd felt normal and like an adult in control of what I did. Drinks and girl time certainly gave me a taste of a newfound freedom outside the mansion. With our plates stacked aside, the waiter approached our table to remove them and sat down the black leather bill, pad folio. When I opened it to place the cash inside, a hotel key was inside with a note that read:

*Hey, pretty lady!*

*Here is my room key if you decide to join me for dessert. If not, I'll understand. However, I'm hoping you do. By the way, your meal has already been paid, but don't tell your friend. Play the game. See you soon! xoxo*

*Lenox*

Flustered Lenox made my temperature rise provoking me to take him up on his offer. I discreetly removed the room key cuffing it in my hand, sliding the padfolio back to the edge of the table.

My motion to rise from the table prompted KK to do the same as we hugged and agreed to text each other within an hour just in case my cousin decided to pop up again. We went our separate ways. She headed to the spa and me to Lenox's room. The quick elevator ride from the lobby the fifth floor brought back those butterflies I once felt before.

I inserted the plastic key card cautiously entered not sure what to expect upon my entry. The first thing I spotted was a white tray filled with chocolate covered strawberries with a note that sat on the table. Lenox had been patiently waiting in the king-sized bed shirtless, exposing his chiseled abdomen.

"It should be a shame that yo ass is so damn fine right now," I managed to say while mesmerized.

"Shit Gucci Queen you're out here hurting these females' feelings. That dress is hugging you just right ma. Now come let me take it off so that we can reconnect."

I laid my coat on the back of the chair, placed my clutch on the desk, and then slipped out of my boots. Lenox's pretty browns never left from off of me as I crawled under the covers with him. Lenox held me in his arms, and then without warning an overwhelming emotion swept over me. Justin suddenly popped in my head, which caused me to cry. It was so embarrassing, but I couldn't control what was happening.

"What I do, ma?" Lenox questioned out of concern. The worried expression on his face made me reassure him all was good.

"You didn't do anything. I had a flashback about my fiancé who was killed back in 2014. He was my first and haven't been with another man ever since. I didn't mean to ruin the mood, sometimes shit happens," I stated without regret.

"It's all good, ma. You can cry ain't nothing wrong with it. This is the first time you've revealed a vulnerable side."

Lenox leaned his head down and kissed my forehead then cuffed me even closer under him. His soft kiss and warm embrace made me feel safe and ready to explore what he had to offer me. I took my free hand and reached to feel how hard his manhood was before letting him know I was ready to play. *Damn, he working with a monster,* I thought as I felt my pussy throb from the anticipation of penetration.

"You ready for me to take you on a journey of ecstasy?" he asked then licked his lips.

"Yes!" I exclaimed then leaned in to kiss his luscious lips.

It didn't take long for him to get on top and ease inside of me. "Ahh," I exhaled from the quick pinch I felt. The entire time I prayed he didn't split me open or cause damage. Eventually his motions in and out grew warm and comfortable. All of those sexual pleasures from before came rushing through me at once. I climbed on top of Lenox; I wanted to try my riding skills out with him. By the time we finished I was convinced his dick was made of some sort of magic. We laid facing one another as we cooled off as the sweat trickled down my stomach.

After a while, my left arm grew numb, so I shifted off it and slipped out the bed to retrieve my phone. It had been on vibrate, so I was kind of nervous to check it as I unlocked it with my thumb. KK had sent a message two minutes prior prompting me to zip into the bathroom to read it.

**KK:** *Girl you don't know what you missed out on. This spa gave me life lol.*

**Me:** *Dude, you scared the shit out of me. I thought you were texting because of my cousin or something. LOL. I'm glad you enjoyed it. Where are you now?*

**KK:** *Slowly getting dressed. You better be doing the same thing.*

*We gotta leave out them doors together just in case we got eyes watching.*

**Me:** *I know. I'm about to take a hoe bath right fast and slip on my clothes. Text me again in ten minutes.*

**KK:** *Not a hoe bath, LOL. Girl, you're crazy. Alright, get yo ass together and meet me outside the spa doors.*

**Me:** *Gotcha. See ya in a few!*

I exhaled while setting the timer for ten minutes then quickly proceeded to wash up before Lenox suspected I was on something shady. When I emerged from the bathroom, Lenox stood by the mini fridge naked, yellow ass cheeks exposed as he drank from a bottle of water.

"Nice buns," I joked catching him off guard. He turned my way giving me a visual of his meat stick. Clean and shaved in the crotch region, his dick looked even bigger, as it lay to the left.

"From that eye expression, I assume this view is better for you. I sure as hell am enjoying what I see," he confessed.

I forgot I was naked or the fact that I needed to get dress and leave before KK came looking at me. Something about that man threw me off, his charm and finesses got the best of me each time. I still can't believe I slept with him so soon, but it is what it is, life was too short not to live a little.

"Aye, I gotta meet my girl downstairs and time is almost up. Otherwise, you know I'd be down for another round. My body feels so alive again. I guess that swim last night helped." I engaged in small talk while slipping into my panties, bra, and dress.

"Let me zip you," he demanded, moving behind me. He felt me up before eventually zipping my dress.

I quickly rushed back to the bathroom to fix my hair, which was disheveled all over my head. I wet my hands a few times slicking my hair back to make it presentable then joined Lenox again.

"Alright, I gotta roll out. Thank you for a great time, we gotta do it again soon. I'm heading out of town for a few days with my cousin so maybe afterwards."

"Looking forward to it," he responded as he assisted me in slipping on my coat.

*Beep! Beep! Beep!*

Sounds of the timer prompted me to move fast like the energizer bunny. Lenox guided me to the door not wanting to let me go. Lord knows I didn't want him to either, but I knew KK was waiting for me in the lobby.

"Alright turn me loose boo, my girl waiting for me. Thanks again for an incredible midday fuck."

In stride, to the elevator, Lenox stood watching until he lost sight. In the elevator alone, I couldn't believe what we had just done together. Almost like losing my virginity all over again, my body felt different.

"Lani, over here," KK caught my attention waving. In surveillance mode, I tried scanning our surroundings in search of one of my cousins or uncles bodyguards. Ain't no way he let me out the house without a pair of eyes following.

"Girl, you are glowing! How was it?" I quizzed curious to know for next time.

"Fantabulous! I'm refreshed and loose. Honey, the masseuse, did wonders on this body of mine. You gotta try it next time when you are not getting ya freak on," KK voiced, causing laughter between us. In motion towards the door side by side, we exited out the automatic doors while retrieving our ticket to give the valet attendant.

"Well, I had a ball today catching up. Thanks for participating in my adventure today, almost like high school fun. Take care and hit me up."

"I'm so glad we've reconnected. I'll make sure to reach out for another adventure. Oh yeah, don't think you slick either, I need some details on our new friend."

"Be cool girl," I wished her well as we got into our vehicles to go separate ways.

Cruising to the crib, I noticed a car tailing me, but realized it was one of my uncle's guys. I continued to think about Lenox, the smooth criminal, who enticed me right out my panties. I broke my own rule by sleeping with a man who I barely knew.

---

I HAD wet dreams for the next week fucking around with Lenox, and if that wasn't enough, my concentration had gotten thrown off. A short attention span tended to be my best friend since Lenox popped into my life. Hopeful my uncle didn't notice my behavior changes. He'd be quick to blame Lenox or even worse lay hands on him. The last thing I wanted to do was bring trouble to either man. Whenever my thoughts weren't focused on fucking Lenox, they wondered about the possible connection he had to Aunt Ruthie.

I sat on the chaise in deep thought about the future. In my head, I had planned out everything hoping that it worked out. If he's the nephew to the plug that would be great for business even making Uncle K warm up to Lenox. For some reason, I truly wanted to be with him even if my family decided to disown me for my actions. For the rest of the evening, I passed the time by cleaning out my closet, listening to music, and painting my finger and toenails. I tried to keep busy so that I wouldn't think about Lenox.

# FOURTEEN
# LENOX SCOTT

When Lani lay in my arms, I had forgotten the fact her uncle was a possible enemy. Forbidden from seeing each other, Lani disobeyed her uncle's wishes. That's why it surprised me that he let her drive instead of having her cousin around. Furthermore, our discussion about me meeting her uncle came up was weighing heaving on my mental.

Something in the pit of my stomach warned me against it, especially since she was a Kingston. However, OG's words of wisdom prompted me to use the situation to my advantage. Still unsure if the hit on my pops came directly from Lani's uncle, I decided to get as close as she would let me. On the one hand, it was wrong because I had her nose open. She had confided shit to me, and I took advantage. Immediately after Lani left my room, a nigga showered and hit to OG spot then my pops.

Upon returning to my room for the night, I found the housekeeper had left everything spic and span. The instant silence and emptiness got me thinking hard about my newfound relationship. That chick really had me missing her, a sign she had gotten to my heart. One thing was sure. I loved the feeling of being inside of that sweet pussy, but most of all her company. Dirty thoughts made me call her up just hear the sweetness in her voice.

Each time we talked over the phone, I learned something new she liked, hated, or wanted. I also discovered triggers both good and bad. Lani had become my pupil, if not for a long-term partnership, for access to take out the Kingston clan. Before our conversation ended, she informed me of her travel plans. In a way it had been a good thing, I needed a clear focus in an effort to resolve the bullshit.

---

WHILE LANI TRAVELED, I used the time to do some more research as I had a plan to turn the crews against each other. I figured that would help make my job a lot easier to conduct real business with the head person in charge. OG noted he had soldiers ready to put in work, so I hit him up for another face-to-face chat. He gave me the okay to swing by, so I did so within a half hour of our phone call. I proposed that a few of his soldiers went to each of the crew's corners and shoot up shit in an effort to blame the other crew. Young niggas were so trigger happy, and down for revenge that I figured they be dumb enough to kill each other. OG agreed and helped set up the details such as the best time to strike

The more I thought about how I'd fallen in love with the enemy's niece; it hurt in both a good and bad way. It was impossible to choose between my pops or a female and hard to separate feelings from business.

Unable to leave Lani alone, we kept sneaking to see each other, something I grew tired of but continued. We were too old to be meeting up like cheating spouses, but I took it how it came and loved it. In a way, our relationship grew prompting each of us to reveal certain secrets to one another. Lani made me feel so comfortable, which was something that no woman had been able to do in over six years. I too lost the love of my life, but to a monster known as lung cancer.

Five years older than me, Kelly had been the reason for my occupational change. Not growing up with a mother in the home, I believe contributed to my taste in older women. Kelly nurtured me giving me a newfound confidence and outlook on life. She saw past the street thug that others had labeled me to be. Instead, Kelly got to know the gentle, loving man many never would. Living life as a misunderstood black man had me believing that I'd always be the thug my pops groomed me to be. Kelly forced me to realize that I could love my father without being his street puppet. I moved to Blackwater, Wisconsin where we lived together until she took her last breath. Years later, the life I ran from returned me to where it all began in an effort to prove loyalty.

On the younger side, Lani had somehow roped me in adding another layer of complexity to my life. Women are the greatest gift and curse to a man for many reasons known and unknown. As human beings, we can't avoid certain things because of our nature to explore and break the rules. Lani, for example, is a curse because my life could've ended at any moment, yet I took a risk and fucked her anyway. She is also a gift because she woke up emotions inside of me. I let die with Kelly. Lani made me feel loved in a manner unknown to me before. She too had me seeing things differently. Hence, the complex dilemma that was all fueled by my father who decided to go chopping off hands and shit. Nothing but time left me to wonder how shit would pan out.

# FIFTEEN

# KINGSTON JR

Back on the road again to Blackwater, Lani ass was knocked out snoring in the passenger seat. It was early as shit on a Saturday morning, but pops said the earlier, the better. Aunt Ruthie made a decision to become our permanent supplier, and she agreed to help us with the takeover pops had planned. He made it plain during our last debriefing how we were about to make changes on the streets.

"It's good to see you two again! Come right inside," she greeted with a smile.

Similar to the last visit Aunt Ruthie welcomed us into her home once we took off our shoes. Instead of escorting us to the kitchen, she led us to the lower level of the home to what I thought was the basement. During the leisurely stroll, she led us into a small room decorated with horse pictures, figurines, and other items. There were two bookshelves, one filled with bronze, black, and gold figurines of all sizes. The other one was filled with a variety of books. I even noticed a book titled *Scarface Nation*, which sat between vintage horse bookends. It was clear she loved horses, but it left me confused about why the fuck she brought us to the room.

"Don't worry. I got a reason for bringing you down here," she commented as if she read my mind.

"I sure was wondering why we come down here," Lani added.

"This appears to be a boring room full of horses, huh?" she questioned, not taking her eyes off Lani and me. We shrugged our shoulders ready to get the hell out of there. All of a sudden, she tilted the *Scarface Nation* book, and the secret passageway opened.

"I knew that damn book caught my attention for a reason," I blurted then laughed. We have a few in our mansion, but I never revealed that to her.

"Good eye! Come on. Let me show you something that no one gets to see unless they work for me. This my friends, is the way to my candy shop. Follow me."

I glanced at my cousin. First, she winked at me. It was an indicator that we were safe to follow Aunt Ruthie. We proceeded to follow her down five stairs as our feet automatically sunk into the soft, cozy carpet. The lighted tunnel excited me because I wondered what other secrets were inside. Halfway down the hall was a door located on the right side of the way. I couldn't make out anything else as the tunnel went further down.

"That's the escape route that leads to the horse stables and another tunnel to freedom. Alright, what you're about to see doesn't get revealed to ANYONE except your father. Understand?" she questioned in her stern grandma voice.

"Yes ma'am," was our automatic response.

"Welcome to the shop," she pressed the door open so that we could get a better view.

"Talk about a whiteout, this here is crazy," Lani commented.

Her comment referred to the mounds of pure cocaine that sat packaged up on a metal slap along with piles in large tubs ready to be shipped. Aunt Ruthie had that Scarface vibe for real, and it was obvious she could get away with murder undetected.

"I keep business flowing through the Southeastern area and as you can see the supply is great. In agreement to help your father become the main connect, I have a gift for him that I'll give you on the way out."

"This is a slick setup you got here. I can only imagine what other tricks the house possesses."

"Honey, you can get a personal tour whenever you'd like, just say the word and it can happen," she seductively spoke.

"Stop that, ma'am, you ain't ready," I joked.

"I can be the judge of that honey, but only time will tell. Come on. I'll grab that so you two can be on your way. I'm sure you guys have things to do."

"Yes, ma'am we do," Lani uttered.

"Manners cousin," I said through gritted teeth.

"I'm sorry. It's just I need to use the restroom and I..."

"It's okay," Aunt Ruthie butted in quickly. "Come on. Follow me." She led us in the direction we came from, back up the stairs, and gestured to the corner room.

The second that Lani closed the door, I felt the awkwardness as I tried to engage in small talk, hoping to get on the road sooner than later. I tried to avoid eye contact because it was clear Aunt Ruthie was on some cougar type shit.

"So how long have you lived in this town? Until now I never heard of it or knew it existed."

"I've lived here over thirty years. It's not a bad place to reside, as you can see it's the perfect environment for me. Lots of folks have never heard of this little town, that makes business even better. Would you ever relocate to a city like this?"

"Nah, it's not fast enough. I like the city life."

"Sometimes a change in pace could be good for a person. You should consider it. There is plenty of room here. Sleep on it."

Lost for words all I could do was smile and laugh hoping that Lani hurried her ass up so that we could get the hell out. From the time Aunt Ruthie met us at the door, she played an eye game. Almost like eye fucking or flirting so to say, never did an older woman come on to me before.

"Ahh, I feel so much better, thank you," Lani voiced as she approached us.

"You're welcome, suga. Let me grab that package be right back."

"Dude, this lady crazy," I whispered to Lani just as Aunt Ruthie entered the room pulling a small dolly with a Styrofoam cooler on it.

"There are several frozen T-bone steaks inside along with three kilos. I threw an extra one in as a sign of good faith. I have a feeling this will be an amiable partnership. Have your father call me tonight at nine o'clock sharp. Otherwise, we can rap early morning."

"Yes, ma'am, I'll pass the message to him. May I ask why so precise with time?" I probed.

"Chile, my favorite show comes on. I don't allow anybody to interrupt my four hours of *Murder, She Wrote*."

"Say no more, Aunt Ruthie. I understand because my favorite show is *Matlock*," Lani mentioned.

Close to the entrance, I lifted the cooler from the dolly and proceeded to carry it to the truck placing it in the trunk. Eager to get from around old, freaky lady, I nicely encouraged Lani to bring her butt on as I thanked Aunt Ruthie one last time. Afterwards, we got the hell out of dodge, and a nigga had to hit the blunt immediately.

"Man cuz, that old ass lady wouldn't stop hitting on me. Her ass basically eye fucked me the entire time. That shit is wild you feel me?"

"I mean you are the ladies' man," Lani bussed out laughing then snatched the piece of blunt and took a few drags until a small roach was left. She then opened the armrest to spray some air freshener.

"Shit, I might fuck with her ass since she the plug. Cougars need love too. But for real, she a little weird at times. Aye, text KD to let him know that we on the way back," I ordered as I let the weed take its course. In chill mood, the ride went fast and quiet.

WHEN LANI AND I RETURNED, we had been informed of the latest chaos to hit the street. I quickly put the meat in the freezer before I was ordered to go straight to the Situation Room. Big brother KD spoke first. Apparently, shit had hit the fan between the Center Street Crew who felt disrespected by some nigga who approached them. They say he let off a few shots and yelled "*Burleigh Boyz nigga!*" before speeding off.

"Aye, bro did anybody get a good look at dude?" I questioned.

"Hell naw. They asses were too busy ducking like little bitches," KD spat, joking.

"Now could this be somebody trying to start a feud, or just some little punk pissed about something? We don't know. That brings me to you, Jr. and Lay. How are we looking with Aunt Ruthie?"

"Is that before or after her old ass kept flirting with me?" I joked but then got serious. "She is all in and ready to help take over shit. Pops give her a ring tonight around nine on the dot, otherwise first thing in the morning. She sent you a gift with a few steaks."

"Why so specific with times?" he questioned suspiciously.

"I asked the same thing. She said don't anybody interrupt her TV time when her favorite she *Murder, She Wrote* is on. She went on to explain how it comes on from ten p.m. - two a. m., which is her downtime, self-care if you will. That lady is interesting, to say the least."

"Yeah, but she is sweet though," Lani added.

"Listen up. Shit is about to change, effectively immediately, and niggas on the streets are about to act a fool. Once the final arrangements are made between Aunt Ruthie and me, we need to eliminate the Center Street Crew, Burleigh Boyz and anything other crew," pops explained.

Kaine finally chimed in the conversation "How are we doing this?"

"The only way we know how," pops answered. "We will be strategic. Remember we have the advantage now with our own personal plug. My only concern is that cock-eyed ass nigga Deuce."

"Oh shit, his nephew's hand got cut off by Lenny. I wonder how that shit is working out for the little dude."

We continued around the table discussing new targets to eliminate. Pops planned the logistics for his takeover. Our meetings lasted as long as it took for all topics to be discussed, voted upon, or whatnot.

# SIXTEEN

# LANI KINGSTON

The first to arrive in the Situation Room, I noticed the projector screen set up, something that hardly happened. I didn't think anything of it and took my seat per usual. The crew entered not wasting time as KD began the meeting. The damn Pandora's Box had opened within a matter of days and niggas had been dropping left and right. Dope houses started getting robbed even some that belonged to my uncle. Uncle K demanded that I stayed on the home front, and I didn't give him any crap.

Sure I missed my store, but my life was more important, so I did as I was told and communicated with Lenox whenever possible. However, his lack of response gave me second thoughts about our relationship. I almost wondered if I should have slept with him. It seemed like he played me for a cheap lay. When KD brought the video up on the screen, my focus diverted pushing my thoughts about Lenox to the back of my mind.

All seven of us watched footage from the selected locations where KD had new cameras installed. He hoped to catch a visual or gain a lead to who was responsible for the hits. At first, I barely paid attention until halfway through. A flicker between the video feed jumped then suddenly more footage revealed my clothing store. My heart pounded hard as I swallowed, praying Lenox didn't appear, and then boom! A quick snippet of Lenox and me hugged up was there for all to see. I literally closed my eyes and counted to ten as I waited to hear my uncle snap. Although Uncle K was furious, he remained cool as more video played.

"Aye, pause it right there," Kaine ordered, pointing his finger. His discovery had us all focused on the person who everyone could identify except for me.

"OH SHIT!" Jr. shouted out then glanced in my direction as if I was supposed to know what was going on.

"That's Lenny's ass hitting up the spots. Muthafucka," KD added.

"FUCK!" Uncle K expressed, slamming his hand on the table.

Clearly he was pissed off, and it frightened me unsure what the hell would happen next. I remained still in my seat, not trying to give him a reason to snap. Far from dumb, I knew whoever the man was in the video would be dead by the end of the week.

"Boys, it's time to clean the streets. Go start prepping while I have a word with your cousin."

Whenever everyone got dismissed except for me, it spelled out trouble. Still silent as a mouse, I braced myself for whatever came my way. It reminded me of my younger days when he tried to explain the rules of our family. As a Kingston, we never turned our backs on each other no matter what the case.

"I'm very disappointed in you, Lani. Time and time again you do things out of spite, and it must stop. I get it. Being told what to do suck most of the time, however, your last name makes you vulnerable."

"Uncle K, I'm always careful, especially with Lenox."

"What do you really know about him, Ms. Careful?

"Enough!" I snapped lying through my, teeth. The truth was I didn't know shit besides what Lenox told me. I agreed to disagree in exchange to leave the table.

# SEVENTEEN

# LANI KINGSTON

I swam at least fifteen laps trying to relieve the anxiety built up inside of me from the family bullshit. After the whole video footage, my Uncle K was pissed at me for disobeying his orders. Even worse, my cousins had orders to cancel Lenox's father. It almost seemed as if I had been sleeping with the enemy the entire time. However, I couldn't stop the feelings I had for Lenox.

When the music no longer blared through the speakers, I emerged from the pool grabbing a soft towel to pat dry. After I slipped into my bathrobe and shower shoes, I took the stroll back to my suite. Out of habit, I reached for the phone hoping Lenox had messaged me, but there was nothing besides the time on the screen. Disappointed, I should've known better to get involved with him from the get-go. I tossed the phone on the bed and moved to the shower to quickly wash and dress in a pair of sweats and t-shirt.

---

NEARLY TWO HOURS LATER, I laid in bed clean, high, and conflicted in my role in luring Lenox to our mansion. Not wanting to appear desperate and shit I refused to reach out to Lenox despite my specific orders. It had never been my intention to get caught up between any of the mess that had transpired. Lenox had been the first man to knock the cobwebs off my pussy. Mad at myself for letting him talk me out of my panties, I had fallen for his smooth talking approach.

Bored out of my mind, I snatched my phone scrolled my apps to find Wheel A Fortune. I got through three games before I received an unexpected guest. It was the last person I'd expected.

"You got time for an old man?" Uncle K asked with his head halfway in the doorway.

"Nowadays I got nothing but time," I shot back trying to keep my attitude at a minimal. He leisurely walked in glancing around the place with his hands tucked in his pockets. My eyes remained glued to the big body man who had played the role of father most of my life.

"Uncle K, is everything okay? You rarely come this way which means your visit is serious."

He let out a deep sigh making way over to sit at the foot of my bed. I sat up and put my focus on him. Butterflies stirred in my stomach not sure what type of conversation was about to take place. One thing was clear; shit could only get worse from where we stood.

"I just want you to know that no matter what happens I'll always love you and I'm proud of the young lady you've grown to become. As you probably suspect I'm here because we need to chat about Lenox."

"What about him?" He stared at the floor before he placed a hand on mine.

"We gotta take his father out and him if it comes to it. I thought it best you heard it from me personally."

"This is about the man in the video correct?"

"Yes."

"I assume I'll never find a man that will survive. I guess the Kingston name is truly a curse. Why does this continue to happen to me? All I want is to be loved and showed affection. Lenox isn't a bad dude. He shouldn't have to face his father's debts or consequences."

"Unfortunately, that's the name of the game, sweetheart. Why do you think I've been so hard on you growing up?

"Uncle Kingston, please let me—" he interrupted, not letting me speak.

"I want to be fair so make arrangements for Lenox to meet me alone for a friendly chat. Before killing his pops, he needs to know why."

"I'm almost sure he's aware his safety might be at stake. This shit really sucks. Oops, excuse my language," I apologized.

"No, you're right, this shit does suck. This game can put a strain between those you love the most. Always watching everybody's back is exhausting but my responsibility. I accepted the terms with the job. You feel me?"

"Yes, Uncle K. I chat with Jr a lot about everything, and he made me understand the pros and cons of being a Kingston. The loss I've suffered is the result of the game. I just get lonely. I have no friends, no job, not to mention nobody gets me. Lenox has made me feel like Justin used to. That's all I want. I'm owed that at least." I felt myself about to cry, and sure enough, the flow started.

"Lani, you deserve the world, and even though I'm not your father, I want to see you happy. If that nigga is doing that good of a job, then I guess I'll have to reconsider my plans for his yellow, smooth ass," Uncle K reassured.

Instantly a weight lifted from shoulders giving me a warming sensation as I jumped up and hugged him. I didn't care that he hated the acts of affection. Deep down it was apparent he loved me like a daughter.

"Thank you, thank you, thank you," I expressed.

"You're welcome, sweetheart. This doesn't change the fact that his father must die for crossing me. Whether Lenox decides to continue your courtship will be up to him, so be prepared for that. Understand?"

"Yes," I quickly replied, not realizing the truth to his statement until after the fact.

"I'll let you get to bed now. Sleep tight, beautiful. See you in the morning." He kissed me on the forehead.

"Do you want the light on?"

"Off, please. Thanks." He hit the switch then left closing the door behind him. I curled back under the cover retrieving the cell phone. Hard not to think about what was to come, I decided to send Lenox a quick message pouring out my emotions.

**Me:** *Hey you! I'm not sure if you're conducting business or traveling, but we really need to talk. Shit has gotten out of hand, but rest assure that I don't have anything to do with what my uncle and cousins do. Regardless of it all, I still want to be with you, and I'm hoping you feel the same way. I'm not the type of female to sweat a nigga or pursue someone if they weren't worthy of my time. We got a connection that I never thought could exist again. I'm saying all of this to say hit me back. I miss you, baby. xoxo*

I hit the blue arrow to send the message watching for the three gray dots to appear. Nothing, just like the previous times, which discouraged me, so I fell asleep with the phone clutched in my hand.

---

THE NEXT MORNING after a pee run, I slithered back underneath the covers not ready to get up yet. Out of habit, I checked my phone instantly noticing a message from Lenox. He sent it shorty after I'd fallen asleep. Just the sight of his text made me smile yet nervous to know what he thought about my text.

By the time I'd finished dissecting his words, I felt some type of way and contemplated on texting or calling him. In one instant, I needed to hear his voice and laugh, but didn't want to face the reality of him verbally breaking off our friendlationship. Finally, I worked up the nerves to call him trying not to think about my uncle's words. When he answered, shivers ran down my spine. His voice filled that empty spot inside of me. In an effort to release the tension, we expressed our feelings for one another in complete honesty. After a few minutes, our conversation turned from awkward back to our regular tone. Before hanging up, we made plans to see each other, which proved a sign he was still digging a chick.

Hungry as a hostage, I got up slipped on a robe and house shoes making my way to the kitchen. The place was so big that all I could hear is pure silence, but it didn't last long. My cousin Kaine wandered in wearing a dark gray jogging suit with wireless earplugs sticking out from each side.

"Morning, big head," I joked as he grabbed a Fiji bottle from the fridge.

I cracked two eggs in a saucepan while my fried bologna sizzled in a similar skillet.

"It's too early for bologna, cousin."

"Not if it's what my stomach craves," I voiced, answering back.

I'm glad we're alone," he stated.

While I tended to my eggs and fixed a sandwich my face frowned unsure what he wanted to talk about, but deep down though I knew it was about Lenox. I rolled my eyes not ready to hear his shit but turned around and bit my tongue to hear him out. Seated at the island across from one another, his body language spoke to me.

"Cuz, you know how I feel, so I'm not sugarcoating anything. What do you know about dat bright light ass nigga?"

In mid-chew his comment caused me to cough, I damn near choked from his unexpected comment. Petty didn't suit him well. However, his attentions were sincere. I took a few sips of water before answering.

"I know enough. Besides, Uncle K came to me last night, and we had a good chat about that topic. All is good for now, so please leave it alone unless you are instructed otherwise. Lenox is not the bad guy you want to believe."

"I don't know or like him, so he better watch his back. If he's involved in those hits, he is getting canceled out like his pop. Just thought you should be aware," he bluntly warned.

"I'm aware of your feelings. Shit, I'm aware of everyone's feelings, but it's fucked up that no one considers mine. Thanks for ruining my meal," I spat tossing the half of sandwich on the plate and stormed out.

Pissed all over again I retired back in my suite not wanting to be bothered.

"ARGH!" I yelled out of frustration fed up with being confined with men all the damn time. In need of a good laugh, I browsed Fire stick to play the movie *Super Fly* and toked up.

---

OF COURSE, during dinner, I brought up the topic still a little heated from Kaine's comments. I felt it had been time all of them heard me loud and clear once and for all because at the end of the day, it was my life, and I had the right to see who I wanted. Sure to wait until most of the meal had been finished, I drank some water then said what needed to be said.

"Since everyone has basically finished their meal, I need to say something right fast. I'm aware of how y'all feel about me seeing the son of the enemy. At this point, I don't care anymore, better yet I'm not sneaking anymore either. Uncle K, I love you and thank you for all you do, but I'm almost twenty-four years old, and I need space and freedom," I truthfully expressed to them.

Between being shocked and proud, my cousins remained quiet.

I continued, "Now if you'll excuse me, my baby and I have a coffee date with Lenox. My baby was the gun Kaine got me.

Send someone to follow if you dare, but you can't stop me from walking out those doors."

I let out a long, loud sigh no longer feeling weighed down as I removed myself from the table. The men just stared at me, the woman who was fed up and in need of space. Still daylight, I slipped on my Gucci shades and clutch exiting the premises. In that instance, standing up to my family gave me a power orgasm in preparation for Lenox.

---

CRUISING in my Benz on the way to the Iron Horse gave me butter-flies. That nigga triggered the hoe in me, and all I wanted to do is have sex with him and feel his strong tongue. Ironically, when I pulled up to the establishment, the same valet person parked my car.

Ready to experience the best sex that I've had, my eagerness damn near carried me to his room. No long nervous to see Lenox, I removed the key from my clutch and let myself inside. After walking a few steps forward, I found Lenox lay up in the bed. At the moment all of the anger left and had been replaced with lust. I undressed and let him take me to another planet with mind-blowing sex. High off life, Lenox had me right where I wanted to be— in his bed and arms. For the first time, I didn't worry about the time or what my uncle would say or do. Free as a bird, I lived in that moment for as long as possible.

Lenox handled me with care, gentle yet rough, caressed my skin, and stroked my hair, all of the things I longed for with a man. While on his chest, I could feel his heartbeat pump on my cheek. Skin to skin, it amazed me at how fast two strangers connected on a personal level, not to mention sexually. I'd prided myself of being responsible when it came to sex. After all, Lenox was only the second man that I shared intimacy with. Living in the moment with Lenox made me wonder what it would be like if we were together for real. Curious about his answer, I decided to probe.

"How are you doing, boo?"

"Shit, I'm great, trying to wake up from this dream. You're just too damn good to be true. What about you?"

"Same, enjoying this time alone. Guess what I did before I got here?"

"What?"

"I let my family have a piece of my mind then stormed out and came here."

"You did what?" he questioned.

I sat up placing my back against the headboard to face him while I continued.

"Yes. I expressed my feelings about you and how tired of being confined I had grew. They were speechless and probably pissed too. I don't care anymore."

"Damn, you something else, queen. So does that mean you are staying the night?"

"I really want to stay but... You know what, fuck it. I'm staying. Let me send Jr. a text so that at least somebody knows that I'm okay." I slide out of bed, exposing my ass cheeks as I recovered the iPhone 7 Plus from my pocket.

"Your ass is looking perfect girl," Lenox hopped up and slapped my butt while I shot Jr. a text.

I felt Lenox place his lips on each ass cheek before standing upright slowly grinding his manhood on me. Eyes closed I couldn't believe that nigga had not only literally kissed my ass but embraced each second.

"Ahh," I moaned, leaning my head back allowing him to twiddle with my nipples. Even after sweating, the smell of his Dolce & Gabbana cologne remained fresh as I got a whiff.

"So does this mean you ready to go one more time?"

"Just a sec," I said, checking the screen to see Jr's reply.

**JR:** *Cuz, you just decided to snap without warning, huh? I got it, as long as you are good. Be safe and bring ya ass home first thing. Don't make us show up at the Iron House and set shit off. Aye, pops was pissed but proud of how you stood up for yourself. Love you dude!*

**Me:** *How the hell you know where I'm at? Never mind. I'll be home before noon. Love you.*

I put the phone down and turned around ready to play house for the rest of the night with my villain. Loose as a goose that man fucked me up, down, and sideways making me fall in love. He dicked me down so good that my body grew limp and sore. I was book and street smart, but dumb for him.

By one a. m., he went to the vending machine to get us snacks for after our smoke session. Dressed in bathrobes, we stepped out on the balcony to hit the blunt a few times before calling it one.

"Lani, I need to ask a question, and I expect an honest answer in return, okay?"

"What you wanna know?"

"Is this meeting with your uncle a setup? Do they plan on getting rid of me?"

His question almost killed the mood, but I answered as honest as possible.

"In all honesty, he just wants to talk. If he wanted to do harm, it would've happened already. I told you about our heart to heart chat, so I'm certain you'll be safe." He handed me the cigar, shaking his head up and down.

"I'm sure you want to ask me some shit too."

"At first I wondered if you fucked me because of who I was related to, but your actions and vibes have proved different. That short time we went without talking made me feel cheap like you played me."

"Oh wow, I'm not even like that ma, on everything," he responded. He took two more puffs before giving me the almost gone blunt.

"I'm glad we had a chance to sit together and get that shit off our chest. So where do we go from here? Like what are we?"

"Shit, you're my girl. What the fuck you thought? I don't go down on a chick if she's not mine. Now let's get inside and go to sleep," he demanded.

"I'm gonna let you know now that I snore, but I'll do my best to keep it down. Can you handle that, playa?"

"Piece of cake. You should know that it's been a long time since

I've shared a bed, so don't be surprised if you feel my hands touch you."

"I can definitely handle that baby. Aye, is there an extra tooth-brush in the bathroom?"

"That's what I was about to do too. It should be because I brought my electric toothbrush."

We headed to the bathroom to brush and gargle then got into bed as if we were a married couple. So used to being in my own suite, it grew hard to get comfortable, but after the awkwardness faded, Lenox held me. His security and embrace made me not want the moment to end. While in his arms secure, my uncle's words echoed in my head about Lenox's father dying. I blocked it all from my mind not wanting to think about the messy situation to come.

---

MY APPEARANCE WAS apparent of an all-night fling no matter how I tried to hide it. Returning home after the way, I stormed out got me to wondering if there would be consequences. Either way, Uncle K deserved an apology along with an update on Lenox. I drove my truck into the garage hoping to sneak a shower before seeing my uncle. One last glance in the mirror, I went on a hunt to find him. During that time of searching for him, the faint smell of weed grew stronger when I passed the ganja. Not sure who was in there, I entered ready to get stoned. Surprisingly Uncle K sat indulging in a fat ass joint as Bob Marley kept him occupied.

"I didn't expect to find you here of all places. May I join you?"

"Come on in, niece." He patted a spot on the sofa next to him.

I sat down inhaling the smells. Not sure if he wanted to hear what I had to say, I tried it anyway. "Lenox will be here promptly at six per your request. I refrained from disclosing any other information."

"Good job, grasshopper. If shit is meant to be, the two of you will make. Otherwise, we kill him too."

Uncle K took two deep drags then passed it to the left in my direction. Only able to tolerate a few puffs, his words haunted me too bad. I prayed nothing happened to Lenox or my family in the process. Suddenly, I felt sick to the stomach in need to lie down. Not sure why I politely excused myself, rushing to get in bed. In a comfortable fetal position, the pain eased allowing me to close my eyelids.

EIGHTEEN

# LENOX SCOTT

It pained me to ignore all of Lani's calls and messages. However, she had my head clouded, and I needed to focus. Life and death had been the only concern of mine because of my father's actions. Instead of making a situation better, he fucked it up worse, which had in return put a wedge between Lani and me. Not able to see her, feel her, or smell her tore me up inside. It also added to my frustrations on how to handle her family. In traffic most of the day, a nigga was dead tired by the time I made it back to the hotel. I stripped out my clothes, washed the day's troubles away, and dressed in a pair of black joggers.

Damn near midnight; I retrieved a pre-rolled blunt and BIC lighter from my luggage. In need to stimulate my mind, I stepped out on the balcony to enjoy the illicit plant for a good five to ten minutes. When I got settled in the bed, my phone vibrated serving as a sign. I forgot to turn the ringer back on. The screen lit up causing me to notice a long message from Lani.

"Fuck!" I yelled, battling on whether or not to read it. I unlocked the phone using my thumb, pressing and holding the green message logo. I eyeballed each word receptive to how she felt. Torn between love and loyalty was a fucked up thing, both could get me killed.

**Me:** *Queen, shit has been rough no lie. My bad for not hitting you back. As you can understand my position, we don't get to choose our parents or family, but you know how the ancient proverb goes, "Blood is thicker than water." Keeping it one hundred, I caught feelings for you too, although it was not my intention. Having a woman in my life proves to be difficult, and our situation is proof. Maybe we can chop it up to get on even ground. Only time will tell until then be well.*

I sent the message and hit the lights calling it a night not sure what to expect from those who might want me dead.

---

UP by six-thirty the following morning, stomach rumbles woke me along with the urge to take a leak. Half an hour later, room service delivered breakfast with a newspaper on the side. Peace and quiet served my mind, well sort of, like the calm before the storm. In mid-chew on pancakes, double vibration prompted me to get up from the desk to snatch my phone off the nightstand.

"Good morning, queen! I hope you slept well." My small talk gave me time to sit back down and put her on speaker while I ate.

"I slept okay. Better now that I hear your voice. What about you?"

"Same. If you read my message then you know I'm conflicted as fuck. I miss you, us, but this family beef has put a strain on shit. I've played tug of war in reaching out to you in case yo people on some setup up shit."

"Given the situation, I understand your position as you understand mine. As I said, I don't have control over how my family handles business. What I feel for you is real, and the time we've spent together was real too. I'm not that type of grimy bitch to set you up. It's not my style. My uncle and I actually had a chat last night, and I poured out my feelings. He wants to have a sit-down, hear you out, and vice versa. This is in no way a setup tactic. It's a legit meeting between two grown businessmen with similar goals."

I listened to Lani speak, and my heart knew her words were sincere, but my gut quivered with a hint of doubt. On the one hand, that was my original goal, but on the other, trust had been something that I had to give sparingly.

"Lenox, are you there?" Lani's voice sounded in my ear.

"Umm, yeah, my bad, I'm just in deep thought. That's something I definitely need to sleep on that. I'll have an answer for you no later than sunrise tomorrow. In the meantime, we should have face to face ourselves overs a fat ass Judy's burger. What you think about that?"

"Hell yeah, I'm down for a burger. Maybe if I'm lucky you'll give me something else that's fat," she expressed lustfully.

"Alright now, don't start nothing. It's too early to be this hard. Aye, you think it's possible to come to see me?"

"I don't know, but I'm sure as hell gonna try," she joked.

"Alright, queen, stay sweet. Talk soon." I wished her well before disconnecting.

Finished with breakfast, I sat and just thought about how shit transpired into the drama that I'm involved in. Lani's mentioning of her uncle's request for a sit-down resurfaced once I had a chance to actually process it. There was a 50/50 chance shit would work out in my favor, or I'd suffer death by the hands of the Kingston Crew. Either way, the game had finally caught up with me. In need of advice, I hit OG up to request a visit, and surprisingly he answered and told me to slide through.

Half an hour later, I pulled up to his spot similar to before and headed to the basement. Not wasting time, we got right to the point updating him on some of the shit that took place. Once I explained the new dilemma in great detail, he provided the feedback that I'd needed to hear. His old school advice usually had merit.

"Damn nigga, you got more problems than a fool going to jail. I understand why you left this crazy-ass city. First let me ask, what do you want to do?"

"OG, this chick got me wanting to risk it all. I tried to use her, but my heart won't let me. I don't know what to do, man," I confessed.

"It happens every once in a while to the best of us. Do you believe she's sincere or a setup?"

"That's the thing. I'm not sure. My gut and heart believe her, but my mind refuses to let me off guard."

"I'll tell ya. The shit women do to us, they'll never understand," OG blabbered.

"Well, we're supposed to hook up for some fun, so I should be able to decide then. This shit just crazy not to mention fucked. How does one choose love or loyalty, pops revenge or happiness? I hate being put in these types of situations."

"Sins of a father are a bitch youngin', but you'll survive. Play your cards right and always rely on your gut. Even the best of the best go through things but prevail. Remember my boys are trigger happy if should need them."

I couldn't help but wonder why OG kept pushing his boys on me as if he wanted to go to war. In assessment mode, I nodded my head yet remained silent. All my life he'd been a stand-up dude with no reason to be grimy, but shit, Kane killed Abel, Brutus killed Caesar and Judas betrayed Jesus, all were fucked up situations. Saved by the buzz of my phone, I answered quickly not bothering to screen the call.

"What's good? This is Lenox."

"You sound so damn sexy right now! I'd love to see you later for a bite if you catch my drift," Lani lustfully hinted.

I was about to grin and grab my dick but remembered where the hell I was at, so I tried to play shit off. "Umm, yeah, that sounds good. I actually could use some help in that department. Let me hit you back in about five minutes," I insisted.

"Are you still at the Iron Horse?"

"Yes, I am."

"Cool. I can't wait to ride your horse. I'll be waiting for your call, boo."

"Damn. Okay bye," I said quickly then hung up.

"That chick is a bad mama jama," OG commented followed by laughter.

"What you mean?" I tried to play the shit off, but his old ass read my facial expression.

"Ole girl got you blushing over there. It's all good. Go handle business youngin'. Be careful," he added.

"Fa sho. Let me get on out of here and see what she wants. Be smooth, my dude." OG saw me to the door locking up behind me.

I hit Lani back in the car before driving off to follow up on her visit. Our arrangements had been set, but I had to give her an answer about meeting with her uncle. Meeting on their turf served as a disadvantage. However, the overall goal to squash beef was worth a try. Not to mention I had been ready to get back to my regular schedule. Living out of a hotel had been cool, but I missed my own house.

---

A FEW HOURS, later Lani entered the room with the key she was given the last time. I was ready to tear that ass up in the bed with just a pair of boxers on scrolling the channels on the TV. A visual of her made it clear that she had me. I let her entice me. As she removed each article of clothing, flaunting herself, my baby was a snack.

"You're naughty, fine, smart, and have bomb pussy. It doesn't get no better than that. Give me some suga." I puckered up.

Lani and I shared a night full of sex, and her ass was hot to trot, giving me the pussy any way I asked to have it. Sexually we took care of each other, filled the craving to get what we wanted. Afterwards, I needed to pick her brain, get an idea where she stood, and see if she truly could be trusted. That night turned out to be the best night I'd enjoyed with a woman in years. When she confirmed she'd spend the night, it was music to my ears. That woman had officially put a curse on me because it was a wrap. She was my woman.

Around five o'clock that morning, I got up to drain the snake but was unable to nod back off. Instead, I laid and stared at Lani who slept peacefully in the nude. Not sure what I did to deserve her, it was my mission to keep her no matter what it took. The wheels in my head began to turn as different scenarios played back.

---

DURING THE DRIVE UP the long driveway, I made it to the gates of the mansion. That shit was lavish as fuck, that cartel type of living. I noticed at least three men dressed in all black on patrol duty. I whipped out my phone to let Lani know I had arrived. Needless to say, everyone in the residence knew it too. A bright ass spot lot shined in my face causing me to instantly throw the palms of my hands up to block it from my eyes. Just as the phone rang, a voice spoke from the black outside intercom system.

"State your business, nigga?" a male voice announced.

"I'm here to see Lani. My name is Lenox, and she told me to come here at six p. m."

"Don't no nigga pull up to these gates asking for my little cousin. I advise you to back on out and enjoy your evening before it's your last one, G," the man behind the intercom warned before the spotlight turned off.

I wasn't sure who the fuck that was behind the intercom, but a nigga started to push buttons with that bullshit. Not sure what type of games Lani was playing, a nigga had business to handle. To avoid a situation from escalating any further, I decided to leave but my phone rang again, it was Lani. I held the phone and let it ring before finally answering.

"Yo. What's going on?" I asked trying not to take out my frustrations on her.

"Lenox I can see you outside from the camera in my room. I'm on my way down because obviously, my cousin plays too damn much. Please excuse my cousins. They all treat me like a five-year-old."

"In all honesty, I understand. However, his threats were not needed. Are you sure that I should be here? I really don't want any smoke with your people."

"It's cool. My uncle actually wants to sit down with you and discuss business. Trust me you will walk out alive and unharmed, I promise," she assured me.

Her eyes didn't lie, so I proceeded with caution all the while it was all a part of my plan to get inside. Up until that point, no one knew where the Kingston's laid their head, and from their set up a nigga understood why. From the outside, the place looked like a legit business building to anyway driving past on the highway. Lani strutted alongside me, the smell of cocoa butter and sweetness seeping from in her direction.

"Stay cool and calm when we enter," she warned as the doors grew closer.

"I'm always cool, queen. I just hope your cousins do the same because we can throw hands at any time," I warned.

"Oh boy, y'all and this territory shit is ridiculous, I swear," she scoffed.

Lani opened the doors as a big body man stood on the balcony of the double staircase. He puffed on a cigar as he waited for our arrival. I watched as he made way down the steps to approach us. He sized me up without revealing emotion. I did the same, standing tall, shoulders back, and not displaying weakness.

"Uncle K, this is Lenox. Lenox, this is my uncle. If you'll excuse, I'll let you two be alone to discuss business," Lani stated. She squeezed my hand before hesitatingly stepping away. I tried my hardest not to gawk at her as she sashayed up the staircase.

"So, you're the little nigga who got my niece sneaking around and shit, huh? I told her to stay away from you, but of course, she didn't listen."

"With all due respect sir, Lani is a grown woman and should be able to see who she wants. However, I do understand where you're coming from. My fault," I apologized.

Quietly he gave me one last glance over then signaled for me to follow alongside him. Hands in pocket, I wiped my palms as my nerves remained faint. Strolling through the many elegant rooms, we came to a set of ceramic stairs that led to the lower level. Located to my left was a door-less arch-shaped room with a medium sized basket posted outside of it.

"That's for all electronics and weapons," he sternly commented.

"What?" I questioned.

"This is the Situation Room where only discussions take place, nothing more or less. You're safe for now. Trust me."

He gestured to the bucket as I hesitated to place my phone and two .9mm inside of it. A nigga felt naked as fuck, but my goal to keep more bloodshed from happening probably wouldn't happen if I didn't hear then man out.

"Help yourself to a drink. Otherwise, take a seat please."

"No thank you. I have to drive," I declined, taking a seat facing the entrance of the door. While observing Kingston's movement, he took a seat directly across from me not saying one word.

"Let's clear the air before we handle business. What are your intentions with Lani since you disregarded my request?"

"Mr. Kingston, truthfully, Lani is a special young woman who I never had plans to fall for, but that was before we got to know each other. My intentions are to continue our relationship regardless of what happens."

"Is that so?" he remarked, stroking his facial hair not loosening his stare. "Even if it means someone you love might lose their life?"

"Listen, I'm not sure what type of riddles you're trying to pull. I'm here because Lani asked. I don't know how you handle business or why it's a bounty on my pops head. Be straight up with me. Why am I really here?"

"Finally we get to the reason for your visit, Mr. Scott. Your father committed some egregious crimes against me that cannot be forgiven. I let him slide for taking a machete to that entitled punk ass kid."

"He came clean about that to me already. I'll admit pops is short-tempered."

"Your father and I did business back in the day. I never had a problem before, which makes things more complicated. I got something for you to view before we continue," he claimed.

Skeptical my patience was running thin while he pushed play on the projector. Focused on the screen, I didn't understand why until I recognized my father in action. Beyond pissed and hurt, my pops told boldface lies about the beef he had with the Center Street Crew. Kingston Sr. shed light on a few things that I had been left in the dark about by my father. Shit, I was even taken aback when Lani and I made a cameo on the screen.

"Do you understand why he must pay? Rather tell you, I wanted you to witness it for yourself. Blood is thicker than water, so do what you have to do. Lani has grown fond of you so as I promised her, you will walk out unharmed. I can't guarantee what will happen after you leave."

Unable to believe the shit that I learned tonight, I had no words that could describe how stupid I felt.

"Mr. Kingston, I respect you as a businessman, but most importantly, for not sugarcoating shit. This entire situation turned out worse than expected. At the end of the day, I must ride or die with my lying ass father."

"I respect that young blood, and I wouldn't expect nothing different. Lani told me you were a stand-up type a guy. It is unfortunate how certain events transpired causing so much riff raff. I'm not sure how Lani will react to it all."

"She's going to be pissed at both of us for sure. Mr. Kingston, I'm clueless on how to move ahead. Any advice before I exit?"

"Listen, women are complicated, especially my niece. She is a piece of work. However, she's worth it. Given our conversation on business, we've concluded your visit.

I shook the hand of the misunderstood man, Kingston Sr., leaving his home with a better understanding of how he conducted business. A lot of the shit OG disclosed to me had clouded my judgment. During my departure, I remained cool up until I climbed inside my car and drove down the driveway. That's when I hit the brakes stopping the car momentarily able to release the frustrations from within me.

"FUCK!" I yelled as I hit the steering wheel with the palms of my hands. "Alright, Lenox keep your cool and go talk shit out with your pops before doing something stupid," I talked myself back to sanity as I continued to drive away.

# NINETEEN

# LANI KINGSTON

Curious, I wanted to know what happened between Lenox and my uncle. When he didn't reply to my text, bad thoughts surfaced. When I checked our security cameras and noticed Lenox's car was still parked outside. I grew scared something had happened to him at the hands of my cousins. No longer able to wait around I went searching for him thinking the worst. From the time that I left my suite rushing down to the meeting room, my fingers remained crossed.

"Uncle K, where is Lenox?" I asked storming in the room only to find my uncle with a phone in hand.

"Sweetheart, I'm sorry, he left in a hurry. He saw the video, honey."

"Shit. Do you think I'll see him again after all of this mess?"

"For the sake of your heart, I hope so, but this is why love doesn't last in this game. We lose those close, which is the one reason I've tried hard to protect you. Life is like a game of chess. Each move planned strategically will get you one step further to your goal or prey. Just be patient. I have faith that things will work out in your favor."

"I really hope so, Uncle K. Lenox means a lot to me. We have grown closer than I originally planned." Before leaving the room, I hugged and kissed him.

Bummed by not knowing anything, my dampened mood made me retreat into hibernation. To pass the time, I blazed blunts, listened to Mary J. Blige songs, and sang my heart out until I eventually cried myself to sleep. I prayed that I got word from Lenox sooner than later just to hear his voice.

# TWENTY

# LENOX SCOTT

Parents were supposed to nurture and groom their children to be better than they were. My parents did a poor job, yet I loved them regardless. After all, we don't get to choose who we're born to. In my case, newfound information about the nigga who trained me to be a hoodlum devastated me to the core. We were two peas in a pot; only now I had to separate myself from him for good.

Although I had been pissed beyond measure, all of that changed the second that I hit the corner of Beacher Street. A dark four-door sedan had just pulled off from the cul de sac near my pops' house. Unsure if Kingston had sent a professional to kill him, I quickly arrived and up pop stairs praying not to find him dead. Upon entering, I promised not to snap until he started playing me like boo boo the fool. Hard to fake my feelings, I strolled in his house to find him drinking a beer in his recliner.

"What the hell wrong is wit you?" is how he addressed me, not bothering to say hello. I bit my tongue and kept walking.

"I had a long day of bullshit. Any beer left?" I asked headed through the house to the kitchen, not waiting for him to answer.

When I returned to the living room, he hadn't budged from his spot in the red leather recliner. Not able to sit close by, I plopped down on the couch several feet away. No longer able to hold my tongue, I turned my head to face him while I spoke.

"Pops, when you called me, I put my life on hold to come to see about yours. I've always had your back through thick and thin."

"And I thank you for it. You've been a great son to me. What's this shit about?"

"How about you tell me why you went around hitting Kingston's spots creating more fucking problems?" His forehead crinkled as if he didn't know what I meant. That expression proved his guilt.

"What the hell are you talking about? Who the fuck you been getting your information from?"

"I watched your old ass in the video footage, so don't try to lie again. Kingston Sr. invited me to his mansion to discuss squashing trouble. Remember that plan?"

"YOU DID WHAT?" he shouted, slamming his beer bottle on the end table as he got out of his chair.

"Pops, you heard me loud and clear. Shit was about to be settled, but yo ass had to ruin it. This is why I left. You don't get it. It's time to sit down, leave the streets along, and enjoy life while you can."

"Are you threatening me, nigga? What are you gonna kill me? You're working with that nigga Kingston now, huh?" "I know, it's that little bitch you've been seeing lately."

"I don't know what's wrong or what type of drug you're on, but I'm about to leave before I say something I'll regret. For the record, her name is Lani, my girl, so watch ya mouth." To avoid further confrontation, I did my best to avoid the man that I no longer knew.

"Don't fucking walk away when I'm talking. I brought your ass into this world, and I'll take you out."

"Go sleep that shit off because you are tripping right now. We can't talk while you're under the influence of whatever that shit is you put in your body. I'm out."

In no way did I want to disrespect my father because he wasn't in his right mind. Therefore, I made another attempt to leave, but he grabbed me like a random in the street. That nigga even socked me in the jaw. Beyond pissed, I popped his ass back in self-defense, of course, and it even stunned him too. In that instance, we begin to fist fight like two random men on the street. Never in my wildest dreams did I imagine having a fucking fistfight with my father. Finally, as a sign of retreat, he stopped tussling and then darted to the back of the house. I took that chance to empty the almost brand new bottle of beer that I no longer craved.

I felt a vibration on the hip but didn't bother checking it due to the current situation. Suddenly a sick feeling hit me, my stomach balled up, and hair on the back of my neck stood. In a matter of seconds, shit went from bad to worse when pops returned with a Beretta .380 in hand. Rage filled his eyes, and his stance was a bit wobbly. He had a killer stare that served as a warning that danger was near. In a smooth motion, I eased my hand on my baby, ready to let off a round if necessary.

"Pop, you really gonna shot me? I'm your fucking son. You don't have to do this—" I pleaded as he raised his right hand aiming the pistol in my direction. Out of survival instincts, my finger squeezed the trigger letting off two rounds in the center of his body.

*POW! POW!*

The sound of two shots went off causing my father's body to drop where he stood in the middle of the kitchen. I stood holding my .9mm all fucked up in the head, in shock of what I did. Tears clouded my vision, as I remained in a statue state filled with mixed emotions unsure of what to do. I didn't want to leave his body in that manner. However, my loyalty had ended. I tucked my piece before getting the fuck out of the house. When I stepped outside, I expected police patrol cars to pull up. However, there was no sign of anyone. Left with no other options, I drove away, not looking back. I drove to the Iron Horse in need of a plan before leaving the city for good.

The first stop I made was to the hotel bar in need of something super strong. The bartender hooked me up with four shots of Jack, and in return, I tossed him a Franklin before vanishing to the elevators then my room. I removed my gun placing it on the stand before I threw myself on the bed. Staring up at the ceiling took me back to my teenage years. Silently reminiscing on the past, I slipped into a deep sleep.

---

THE NEXT MORNING sleep and a hot shower brought me back to the new reality as bits and pieces of the previous night flashed. Almost sure that Lani hated me, my love for her wouldn't allow me to give up on us. After doing nothing but reflecting on the incident, I came to my senses and wanted to go back to Kingston's mansion praying to seek approval to move forward.

When I found my phone, I hit her with a brief text requesting to make another visit. I promised to explain everything to her if she was willing to give me another chance. Grateful she agreed to assist me as I quickly dressed, packed, and checked out in route to see her.

Forty minutes later, I arrived in their driveway as the black iron gate opened allowing me to proceed. More at ease this time, my eagerness to enter the mansion and see my queen kept me antsy. I stepped out the Lexus and took the short stroll up the doors unsure of who would answer this time. All of a sudden, a nigga was all teeth when Lani opened the door leaping into my arms.

"You had me so fucking worried, nigga," she hissed before wrapping her arms around my neck.

Our embrace had been the best feeling in the world since the outcome could've been very different. Not wanting to let her go I carried her inside as she slammed the door. We shared a very intimate kiss until her uncle appeared. I quickly put Lani down not wanting to get on his bad side again.

"Mr. Kingston," I acknowledged, extending out my hand.

"Nice to see you, son," he reciprocated the handshake. When Lani told me you wanted to meet again, I figured out why. Come on. We have a discussion to have."

Alongside him, we strolled to the room where I firsthand witnessed my flesh sign his death threat. Similar to before, I removed my pistols and phone placing in the box. However, I didn't expect to find three dread heads already sitting at the table. I recognized two of the three men who mean mugged me.

"What up, light skin nigga?" Kaine shot a smirk with his comment.

"Behave," his father warned with a stern look. "Lenox here has something he'd like to share with us. Show him respect while he does it," Kingston Sr. warned.

"Thank you. First off, I don't want beef with any of y'all. I came here to clear the air and say my peace. Last night I left here, I confronted my father and shit went left fast. That nigga pulled a gun on me, and in self-defense, I had to lay him out. I assume this leaves us on good terms?"

"Prior to our chat we are no longer enemies, but if you hurt my niece, you will join your pops. Got that?"

"I wouldn't expect it any other way, sir."

Once I informed them of the situation in regards to my father's untimely death, all beef had been officially ended. The next order of business included apologizing to Lani. I shot her a text to come to find me so that we could talk privately.

"You survived the Kingston sit-downs," her voice projected from behind me prompting me to turn around.

"This place is huge, baby. It's like living in a museum. When you talked about this place, I didn't realize your uncle had a bank like this. Anyway, can we go somewhere to talk?" She grabbed my hand leading me in the opposite direction to a place unknown. We entered a large lounging room decorated with a 1920s feel to it. The beautiful woodwork, fireplace, and furniture décor brought a sense of serenity.

"We can sit here and talk without being interrupted." She led me to the couch. Silent, I just watched the beauty within her beautiful face.

"I need to tell you something. The night your uncle showed me the video of my father, I truly believed my life would end. When it registered what had happened, I couldn't face you in that condition. Hurt and angry was no way to step to you. Therefore, I went to confront my pop."

"What happened?"

"Long story short, he pulled his gun on me, and I killed his ass to save my life. Matter of fact, just before it happened, my phone went off, but I ignored it. Had I answered my ass might be dead. Now, do you understand why I had to be distant?"

Right then I watched a single tear fall from her right eye. She expressed emotion as if she felt the pain that I too felt. At that moment, I knew Lani was the one I wanted and needed to be with for life.

"Marry me," I blurted. Life proved to be unpredictable, so I wanted to give her my last name.

"What? Are you serious?"

"Listen, I love the fuck out of you and can no longer wait to spend each day together. I'm not sure how the guys will react, but I don't want to wait."

"I love you. Wow, I can't believe the words that slipped from my lips. Too bad we can't slip away for some fun."

"When you are my wife, we can do anything we want together without needing approval, Mrs. Scott."

"Sounds like music to my ears! Kiss me, handsome." She puckered her lips pressing them against mine.

From that day forward, I gained a family eventually winning the approval of her cousins, but most importantly, her uncle. In the process, I learned that my Aunt Ruthie had been their secret supplier. Although I planned on leaving the game alone for good, Kingston requested I get my hands dirty every once in a while. Of course, I agreed.

FEBRUARY **2019**

I placed soft kisses on Lani's lips urging her to wake up for a dose of morning loving. In bed together as the sunrise shining brightly into our room, I thanked God for allowing me to be free finally. Life had definitely thrown me a bunch of fucking lemons, but as a product of the hood, I made the best of it all. The killing of my father played tricks in my head for a long time, but the more time Lani and I spent together, that old life faded from my memory bank. As an official couple, her uncle gave his best wishes to us moving in together a few doors down from the mansion.

Our wedding started the beginning of a new me in a loving and family orientated way. I kept my home in Blackwater because that served as a hideout spot in case shit hit the fan, and also because Aunt Ruthie requested we visit once a month. She and Lani became super close, and I believe she had finally found that woman and motherly figure she longed for since a child. Eventually, the family resumed their daily duties while Lani and I tried to figure out how to reveal the surprise of an addition to the Kingston family.

While Lani was out with Jr., I hit up OG; I hadn't spoken to him since that shit went down with my pops. After the initial shock of finding out about the baby, I wanted to chop it up with him. It surprised me that he answered during the first call, which almost never happened, and gave me the okay to stop by. I scribbled on a piece of paper and left the note on the fridge where Lani would see it. I grabbed my keys and walked out the door that was connected to our garage. I hit the garage button as it opened; I hopped inside my ride, slowly backed out and drove away. Little to no traffic early Saturday morning it didn't take long for me to pull up at OG spot.

I approached his stairs and couldn't help but notice the for sale sign hanging. By the time I hit the top step OG had opened the door for me. When I entered there were boxes scattered everywhere, and it looked like he was leaving soon.

"C'mon in light skin," joked.

"Damn, it looks like you on the way out," I commented.

"It's time for a change in scenery you feel me? Aye, I need to wrap with about ya pops," his tone changed.

"Yeah, we do," I responded and followed him to the basement. On the way down I wondered what he knew. *How the fuck do I tell OG I killed my father? That shit was for real self-defense,* I thought not ready to relive my actions.

"I'll ask you one time, and I expect the fucking truth," he spat.

Before he could ask the question, I decided to address the elephant in the room. I needed to get the shit off my chest. I faced him like a man and went into details of how shit went down. As I explained, OG studied my face and body language in search for deception. I understood where he was coming from, but there was no reason to lie to him.

"Why the fuck didn't you hit me up?" he spat.

"I wasn't in my right mind. After that, I drove to the Kingston estate to handle business."

"I went to see your pops that night to discuss the Kingston situation. When he didn't answer the door, I went inside and found his body on the kitchen floor. It fucked my head up to find him like that," OG confessed. He took a seat and continued. "I had a cleaning crew come through and do a sweep to dispose everything."

I took a seat next to him and slumped over placing my elbows on my knees. Out of nowhere, a wave of guilt rushed through me and in that moment I broke down. "I killed my fucking father. How the hell can I be one to my own child?" I cried out.

"Say what?" OG asked.

"Yeah fam. It happened fast, but after the shit with my pops, I squashed the beef with Kingston Sr. Lani, and I tied the knot now she carrying my seed."

"Yo' ass been moving fast, but I'm proud of you for wanting to do better. You will be a good father as long as you do the work. My crumb snatchers fucked up in the head like me because of my ways. You different young blood, you got a chance to break that fucked up cycle we pass on to our off springs."

"Thanks man, I needed to hear that. Aye, you never told me where you going?"

"I'm leaving the city for a fresh start myself. I got word that my sister in Arizona is getting sick again; fucking cancer is back with a force. They say she got about two years left."

"Damn. I'm sorry to hear that shit. Cancer been taking a lot folks, but it'll be good for you two to spend time together," I sympathized.

"I'm out this bitch by the end of the week. I'm getting too old for this street shit. You feel me?"

"I sure do. I keep my ass in the house watching Lifetime with my wife and shit," I joked as I stood from my seat as we embraced each other with a bro hug. Just before I was about to leave out the door he stopped me.

"Aye, think -fast," he shouted as he tossed me a small prepaid phone. "This is to ensure we keep in touch. I stand on my word, if you run into trouble, hit me up. One luv," OG nodded his head.

"I already know fam! Safe travels," I replied while I crossed the street and entered my vehicle. I drove off knowing that nigga would always have my back no matter what city. It was hard to believe how fast things changed, but grateful for the wisdom I had learned. The talk with OG had me excited to get home to see my beautiful wife. She definitely had become the light of my life.

---

I PULLED INTO THE GARAGE, and when I entered the house, I could hear the television on. When I walked further inside, I found Lani and Jr. in the living room watching *Empire* on DVR. It made my heart smile to see my girl laughing and enjoying life. A big smile crept across my face as I walked over to kiss her on the cheek. Her pregnancy glow made her even more gorgeous than ever.

"Hey baby!" she blushed.

"What up Jr.," I said as we gave each other a fist bump.

"Aye, Lenox, can we chop it up for a second?" Jr. asked as he stood up from the couch.

"No doubt. Baby, we'll be back in a minute," I blew Lani a kiss. Jr. and I walked a few feet and stepped into my office closing the door. Not sure what the hell was going on, my forehead wrinkled in confusion.

"Don't trip, my pops didn't send me," Jr. clarified before he continued. "Pops is sending me to Chicago for a bit to handle some business with my other brother. While I'm gone, I need you to guard my cousin with your fucking life. She told me about the baby. Congratulations."

"Thanks, man! I should've known she'd tell you first."

"Pops won't trip since y'all married. However, you got some big shoes to fill because everybody about to be on ya ass. I digress; I'm leaving in three days and don't know how long I'll be gone. I'm relying on you to keep my cousin protected from danger. We straight?" he questioned.

"I got her believe that," I answered without hesitation.

"I knew you'd understand where I was coming from. Shit started off rocky between us but you good people. If anything jumps off, don't think twice to hit me up."

After the man-to-man chat, we exited my office and went back to the living with Lani. Jr. hung around for another hour before he dipped out. Lani laid in my arms as I reflected on my conversations with OG and Jr. It amazed me how shit had a way of working itself out in the lease expected ways. I spent the rest of Saturday night cuddled up with my wife as I placed my hand over her stomach. I couldn't believe a thug like me had officially become a changed man.


THE END

CPSIA information can be obtained
at www.ICGtesting.com
Printed in the USA
LVHW041508171019
634537LV00003B/465/P